A Place in His Heart

A Place in His Heart

By: Donna Whitaker

A Place in His Heart

Published by:
Oak Tree Publishing PO Box 1373 Somerset, KY 42501 USA

'We help grow your project into a mighty oak.'

ISBN: 978-1-7346142-5-1

This is a work of fiction.

Cover Design by: GoodHope Designs by: Sandy Hawk

GoodHopeDesigns1001@gmail.com

Dedication

To my beautiful children,
Sie, Jr., Jennifer, and David

Acknowledgments

Thanks to Editor Carol Cartaino for her guidance in refining my writing skills.

Special thanks to my sister Glenna Drew for her valued and insightful critique.

Love and appreciation to my dear granddaughter Nicole Daley for posing in the photo for the front cover.

Cover design: Good Hope Designs
Photograph of Donna Whitaker by Glenna Drew
Photograph of cover by Griffin Ball

All scripture quotations are taken from the King James Version of the Bible.

CHAPTER ONE

RACHEL gazed out the small window of her cabin, drinking in the fragrance of the newly-honed logs—logs she and hired man Frank had cut from tall trees of this wilderness setting in Stone Valley, Kentucky, that had become her new hope. As she closed her eyes, her mind wandered back nearly two years to the cabin she had shared with Mother and Pa on their farm in Virginia and the first time she had laid eyes on Ransom. It seemed a lifetime ago....

Virginia, October 1792

STANDING BY THE CORRAL, hands gripping the rail and his head nestled in the crook of his arm, John Winslow prayed. Not sweet, tearful entreaties, but desperate prayers wrenched forth in fright and despair.

A hardened man, John stopped praying years ago. He'd found no need for God and now he couldn't calm the uneasy thought that God wouldn't hear him. He knew that he had abandoned God and, feeling unworthy, believed that God, in turn, had forsaken him. The longer he prayed the more helpless he felt.

So, as he waited for news from the cabin…he quit praying.

Finally, as the afternoon shadows drew long, heavy footsteps sounded on the thick grass behind him. He shifted his face and saw Doctor Stone approach, lines furrowing his brow. John straightened, turned, and frowned as well, as fear of the impending news raced through his mind.

“About your wife,” Doctor Stone began, a careful note to his tone, and for a long moment weighed how much to say, how to say it, and how to respond to any reaction he might get from John Winslow, “I’m afraid,” he finally said regretfully, “there’s not much I can do for her.”

Clenching his jaw and gazing stone-faced at the cabin where his wife lay sick, smoke rose from the chimney sending forth its pungent smell.

“How long?” The doctor heard a tinge of guilt was heard in those two words.

Doctor Stone hesitated. “Not long now,” he said, penitent, to be the bearer of bad news. “If I’d been sent for sooner,” he explained, “there might have been a better chance. I’ll stay until—”

“No!” John rasped.

John’s gaze went to the ground and in a quieter tone said, “Rachel and I can take care of things.”

“But, Mr. Winslow, I don’t have any other seriously ill patients pressing me today,” the doctor protested. “I’d like to be here when she—” He broke off as John squared his shoulders and gave a look that defied any further offers of help.

Doctor Stone studied him, thoughtful. John Winslow was a large man, wide-shouldered, black hair, black eyes and if there was any softness in him, it was well hidden. Intimidating, to say the least.

Though the Winslow family had lived on their farm for many years, he didn’t really know them. In fact, no one in Wellington did. On the rare occasions when John went to town, he went alone most of the time. He did not talk about his past or present and when questioned about it in friendly conversation, his inquisitors were often met with a reproving stare. He took care of any business he had, and left quickly, saying little to anyone.

The doctor’s mind wandered to John Winslow’s daughter Rachel stationed by her mother’s cot in the cabin. Take care of things? He didn’t think she looked capable of doing what needed to be done. A small, shy girl with dark hair in need of combing, it was obvious she considered him an outsider. He could tell by the apprehension in her eyes when he approached her. He had seen her kind before. Not many. But there had been a few.

"What do I owe you, Doctor?" asked John, but it was not really a question. Rather, an invitation for the doctor to leave.

"Don't worry about it," Doctor Stone answered, giving a slight shrug. "We'll settle up later."

The doctor turned to leave, then gave his face a quarter turn back. "By the way, I've left some medicine. It won't cure your wife," he explained, "but it will help some with her coughing."

The cabin was hot but Rachel, with sweat trickling down her forehead, kept the fire burning high as she watched her fevered mother, emaciated, sunken eyes closed, wither away before her eyes. Emily Winslow was a tall woman but, to Rachel, seemed so small as she lay there.

"It's just a summer cold that's lingered, causing a rattling in my chest," Emily had protested to John when he asked about taking her to Wellington to visit the doctor. Then, as it persisted, the cold had turned into pneumonia and Rachel, their only child, remained a constant presence by her sick mother.

Rachel seated herself in the rocker by the hearth. Unnerved by the rasping coming from her mother's chest, she got up and moved to the small sideboard that held the basin. She must do something—anything—to occupy her hands.

Dipping fresh water into the basin, Rachel carried it to her mother's side, sloshing liquid over the rim as she went. Setting the pan on the floor, she seated herself next to her mother's cot.

Drawing the blanket tighter around her mother's neck, Rachel leaned over and in a small voice whispered, "Mama, don't leave me."

Emily roused and a tiny light shone in her feverish eyes as a smile touched one corner of her mouth. Always *mother*, Rachel had not called her mama in years.

"Where is the doctor? And where is Pa?" Rachel thought

frantically as she sponged her mother's face then forced water past her lips. She and Mother needed him...needed his strength…needed his reassurance.

Seeking her father for comfort earlier in the day, Rachel found him behind the barn crying. She had never seen him shed tears before and stood transfixed as his shoulders shook with weeping. To spare him the embarrassment of being discovered, she retreated quietly, feeling lost and alone.

Her world was no longer one of carefree abandonment in nature with God's creatures and the tiny bluebells and yellow wildflowers. The flowers had withered with the passing of their season. The woods had changed from deep green to various shades of scarlet, yellow, and russet. Summer had faded into fall and fall was being swallowed up by winter…and then before evening came….

Mother was gone.

All that evening and the next day, John would not leave Emily's bedside. He held her hand and was as solicitous as though she were still alive as grief unsettled his mind.

Rachel slept little that first night. With her mother lying silent in the next room and her father tossing restlessly about, it was evident her father was not in any frame of mind to oversee the burial. She would have to do it all herself, as well as searching for some appropriate passage from the Bible to say over the grave.

When the sun rose over the hills to the east, she climbed from her bed and, opening the shutters on the window, laid her arm on the windowsill and looked out over the farm. The last of the summer garden had to be picked and preserved before a hard frost set in. The cows needed milking and the horse turned out to pasture. Eggs were waiting to be gathered and wood to be chopped. Nothing had changed. The farm looked the same for all that Emily was dead.

There was no time to mourn and after the milking and tending to the chickens, Rachel spent most of the day digging the grave. Evening was drawing on. The cows needed milking again and the horse corralled before she returned to the cabin.

Standing by the pit, spade in hand, and pausing to wipe her forehead with the back of her hand, she glanced toward the cabin.

Rachel felt desolate and alone and she had never been lonely before. How very strange this feeling.

Returning to the cabin at dusk and lighting the lamp, Rachel put the pail of fresh milk on the sideboard, shed her coat and hung it on a peg.

She leaned against the door and stood transfixed at the sight of her father sitting on the floor beside her mother. The smell of death, although faint, was already in the room.

"Pa," Rachel said wearily, "we have to get Mother ready for burying."

John turned to her with a savage glitter in his eyes.

"*No!*" laid across the air like a whip and Rachel shrank against the door. What she heard and saw touched her with an icy finger of alarm.

As John Winslow turned back to his wife, Rachel realized two things: The man before her was not the same and this was not something she could handle on her own.

Who could she turn to? Certainly not their neighbor Floyd Thompson. She rarely saw him, and he frightened her with his rough ways. And in John Winslow's state of mind, he might very well throw Thompson off the place.

For a few moments, her mind went swiftly down the years and she remembered her mother, quiet, gentle, teaching her scripture and how to pray. She searched her mind for something that might be appropriate for this situation, but those prayers seemed insufficient now.

"What to do—oh, Mother—what to do?" Rachel whispered to her.

But her mother, lying lifeless on the cot, could no longer hear.

Suddenly her heart was sick as she faced her own inadequacy.

"God," Rachel whispered tiredly as she dropped in a chair at the table, "if you can hear me, please show me."

Nothing. Was God not there?

She should eat but was too tired to cook and John had let the fire die down anyway. "Perhaps milk and cornbread," she mused.

Wearily, elbows on the table, she rested her face in her hands.

"What can I do, dear Lord, what can I do?"

A few moments passed by and an idea struck Rachel. She looked up wide-eyed.

Yes, of course! The preacher!

John never allowed his family to attend church. Emily, nevertheless, often told Rachel about church services she had attended while growing up and her descriptions would almost bring to life the preacher's sermons and the songs they sung.

"Will Pa try to stop me?" Rachel asked herself. "Would he even know I'm gone? What will he do to the preacher once he got here?"

Rachel decided this was the only thing to do. She would go to Wellington and seek the preacher's help.

"And I'll do it," she muttered decisively, "whether Pa likes it or not!"

CHAPTER TWO

EARLY THE NEXT MORNING, Rachel saddled her father's horse and headed for Wellington. A little uneasy, she had never been to town by herself, coming with her father only rarely.

The trees, that had offered inviting coolness in the heat of a summer's day, were now a grim reminder of her mother's death as their leaves were detached by the brisk, cold wind and sent skittering across the road.

Nothing felt right with the world. An eerie feeling that some disaster was to come, refused to go away—a feeling, deeper than her mother's passing, as though something was waiting that would try to swallow her up in its thick darkness.

Rachel had never known this type of feeling before. All her life she had been sheltered and made to feel secure and loved and now—anything but that.

Rachel had kept her grief in check, but tears now found their way down her cheeks. "Mother, why did you leave us?" she cried.

She had been so happy and now her world was turned upside down. Her only answer was the howling of the wind and an ominous feeling that her life would never be the same.

Wellington came into view. Seldom seeing anyone but closest neighbors, the thought of riding alone into a town filled with so many people set her heart to thrum a little wildly in her chest.

But she stiffened her spine against her feelings.

Stopping at the livery on the edge of town, she asked warily, "Could you tell me where the preacher lives?"

Some of the townspeople took notice of the strange girl riding down Main Street straddling the horse and were surprised she was alone. Glancing once at them, Rachel quickly looked away. She felt, rather than saw, their stares and felt no boldness to challenge their gazes. She said nothing to their remarks for her only thought was reaching the parson.

Finding the parsonage, she ascended the steps with her heart in her throat. She knocked softly and the door was soon answered.

Rachel felt suddenly small and awkward.

"Are you the preacher?" she asked.

"I am Pastor Jacob Templeton," he answered. "How may I help you?"

"My—my name is Rachel Winslow," she announced, a plaintive tone in her voice, while clutching her coat close to her. With a wave of the hand toward the outskirts of town, she said, "I live a few miles from town and my—my mother died two days ago."

Then, feeling as though she was betraying her little family, she fumbled for the right words, "My father is out of his mind. He refuses to leave Mother and he will not let her be buried. Please—please, come and help."

Jacob stood in the open doorway staring at the hatless girl dressed in pants for a moment as the cold air swept the house. He knew most of the people in the county but did not recall anyone by the name Winslow. Certainly, no one by that name attended his church. Then, remembering his role as pastor, said, "Come in—come in." Ushering her into the parlor he turned and called, "Elizabeth!"

His wife quickly appeared in the hallway.

"What's wrong, Jacob?" she asked alarmed.

After Jacob explained the situation, he hooked up the carriage and both insisted that Rachel ride in the conveyance with them.

Haltingly, Rachel refused. It is not that she meant to be unfriendly, but she could not explain the sense of familiarity and security that riding her father's horse gave her.

It was a short service. To Jacob Templeton, John Winslow had not appeared unhinged as Rachel had suggested, but was only a man in acute mourning. Jacob had finally been able to convince John that Emily would have wanted a Christian burial. The word "Christian" had been the clincher.

Emily was a Christian and the fact that John had denied her the pleasure of attending church struck his heart with a sense of profound guilt that he would carry with him the rest of his days.

Emily had asked little from John in their marriage except, she wanted to attend church. He would have done anything for her, but that. And now, if he could undo the past, he would gladly not only let her go, but go with her himself. But now…it was too late.

The fourteenth chapter of St. John was read, and John mumbled, "That was her favorite scripture."

As soon as it was over, it was apparent John wanted them to leave. He did not invite them into the cabin and moved nervously around intimating silently that their speedy departure would be welcome.

He wanted to be alone. Alone with his memories…alone with his grief…alone with his guilt.

"An odd family," Jacob told Elizabeth as the carriage turned onto the road. He had ministered to many people and learned the signs. Most would want a comforting presence at this time instead of being alone.

"But," he sighed, "I'm a servant of the people and must respect individual wishes." As he and Elizabeth started toward Wellington, he breathed his own prayer of consolation for this man and his daughter in their loss.

But John could not be consoled. Not that he ever cried again, but in the recesses of his heart where Emily had brought warmth…that warmth had been stolen and even Rachel could not melt the numbing cold that followed.

If anything, he lapsed deeper into depression, for when he saw Rachel, he was looking at the image of Emily. Day by day he lay on the makeshift cot that Emily had died on.

In the semi-darkness he would stare unwaveringly at Emily's worn Bible as though by his own volition he could make her appear and he would once again hear her soft, melodic voice reading scripture—and each night when she did not come, he would finally drift off to sleep.

"Could he have truly lost his mind?" Rachel despaired.

As the days blurred together the farm was neglected, leaving Rachel to fill the gap as head of the family. Gone were the days when she was Emily's little girl and John's adorable, frolicsome, carefree daughter.

Waking one frigid morning in January, Rachel found, much to her surprise, that a heavy snow had fallen. She loved the snow and remembered other winters when she had created works of glistening white art while her father looked on in amusement.

Frowning, she thought, "I don't have time to play in the snow. I've got to kill something for us to eat." She had made do, up to now, with the few rabbits she had trapped, an occasional chicken, and the vegetables from the winter garden, but now felt the need for bigger game.

The cabin had grown cold. Rachel shivered while pulling a top over her shift, stuffing it into britches and slipping on her shoes. Throwing some logs into the hearth and taking a poker and scratching at the ashes for live coals, she rebuilt the fire. Pulling on her coat, she glanced over her shoulder at her father sleeping on the cot and took his rifle from the mantel.

"Thank goodness, Pa taught me how to shoot!" Rachel said out loud as she downed a deer. She was an expert shot but dressing the animal was a different matter. She had enjoyed hunting with Pa, but always lost interest when it came time to dress their game. With her hand over her mouth and a shake of her head, she said distastefully, "I can't think of that now."

Wielding the knife without her father's expertise, she applied herself resolutely to the task at hand and as a light snow began to fall, the white snow turned to shades of red.

Rachel was not much of a cook but what she rustled together was, at least, palatable. Even so, John barely choked down a few bites.

Irritated, Rachel stared at her father. He was head of the house—

not she! She looked down at her hands. They were not the hands of a young girl. Not that she minded work, for she did not. She didn't mind the milking and tending to livestock, cooking and washing, but she did mind that he shirked his duty as her father. She minded that logs, dragged in using the horse, needed to be cut and split and should have been stacked months ago.

Her irritation turned to alarm, however, as she watched him withdraw into his own solitary world. And the burly man she loved grew gaunt as the days passed. If only he would go into a tirade and become that loving, blustering father she knew so well!

Unceasing labor was now Rachel's fate. Her small hands were blistered chopping firewood, a grisly task as she was no hand with an axe, but a chore that her father did with ease.

Rubbing fat on them and wrapping them with long strips of cloth brought tears to her eyes, but this was what life dealt her and she had to cope with it.

Often, she thought of Mother and her unflinching strength. Realizing there was now no one with whom she could share her burdens, she resolved to do whatever she had to do. She grew up in a hurry, and just as her hands eventually became calloused, so a shell was hardening over her heart.

She would never be the same again.

CHAPTER THREE

THE DAYS TURNED INTO WEEKS AND THE WEEKS INTO MONTHS. In late March, winter, unwillingly, with a last ferocious ice storm, gave way to the promising smell of spring. A few weeks after that last icy blast, Rachel was busily cleaning up her mother's garden area and wondering how she was going to buy seeds to plant.

John Winslow always had a little money but moved its hiding place from time to time, and just where it was hidden, she did not know.

Rachel contemplated trading a few chickens with their neighbor Floyd Thompson. But Floyd would undoubtedly brush aside her attempts at bartering and question the state-of-affairs at home. And that, she decided, she wanted no one to know about.

Like a sleeping giant come to life, John Winslow suddenly roused from the despair that had held him captive for months, surprised that it was now spring.

Barely sunup, he looked around the cabin inside and out. It had rained and fog hung thick in the air. The horse was corralled, the rooster crowed, but Rachel was nowhere to be found. But then, he couldn't see past the barn in the mist. Picking up a load of wood for the house, he realized that he was physically out of shape.

But no matter. He quickly made up his mind what he would do. He would leave this place with its tormenting memories.

"Where will I go?"

He had no kin to speak of except a couple in Pennsylvania who had raised him. And they were not really kin. Being orphaned while young, they took him in. But he had earned his keep…and then some.

As quickly as he thought of them, he dismissed the idea from his mind. He had no desire to return there.

A memory stirred. There had been talk the last time he had been to Wellington. A scout was in town with news about a party from Bedford County he was to guide to Kentucky come spring. He had said something about some church congregation settling somewhere in Lincoln County.

John had heard of the Kentucky land for years—its promise *and* its danger.

"Yes," he quickly decided as he walked through the door, "that's where I will go. I'll find that scout and join that party."

"But what about Rachel?" he mused aloud, depositing the wood at one end of the hearth. That land was Indian territory and he could not take her there. And chances were, some Indian buck would abscond with her and he would, undoubtedly, lose his scalp in an attempt to rescue her.

"No," he shook his head and said to the air, "'tis best to leave her in Virginia where she would be safe."

A plan formulated in his mind as he paced about the cabin. He had heard Reverend Templeton was a good man of the cloth and realized Rachel needed more than this farm. In his own selfishness, he had kept her isolated from others. But she was nearly a woman now and needed more than his crude ways. Nice clothes, education, and the ways of society were just the things that would change her from the wild creature she is into a lady.

He would have papers drawn up making the Reverend Templeton trustee of the farm and Rachel his ward.

"Rachel's been too long like me," he rationalized. "Emily would be pleased at this decision."

Leaving Attorney Richard Adkins office, John breathed a sigh of relief. It was done. He had signed Rachel into the custody of Pastor Jacob Templeton and his wife Elizabeth. No matter that they knew nothing of his decision. Surely, they would not leave a young girl alone to face the world.

But he realized that convincing Rachel to leave the farm would be no easy matter. It was what she had known all her life and to suddenly snatch her from it would take persistence on his part as her tears would be the only thing that might melt his resolve.

John knew he was a coward for running away, but the memories of Emily, growing weaker day by day, until she finally succumbed to pneumonia's grip, were still too vivid in his mind and for sanity's sake, he had to leave Virginia.

During Emily's illness, John had prayed that God would forgive his past transgression for departing from the faith and spare her life.

"Perhaps," he now briefly agonized aloud, "I've been wrong to do what I've done...wrong in turning my back on God...wrong in running away...wrong in signing Rachel out of my life."

Thinking of Rachel, he shoved aside his misgivings and determined that she would be better off without him. The past few months had proven that. He had been no help to her at all.

And he could not give her what she really needed. Things like education and spiritual training when he felt little need of God himself. She also needed to learn the womanly arts of living amicably among society.

Living on the farm and having little to do with the rest of the world, she had become a little too wild.

"She'll be reaching marrying age soon," he said to the air as he rode towards home, "and she needs to learn social graces and to mingle with the rest of the people of the county."

He frowned. Rachel was pretty, no doubt about it. Her black hair and dark eyes would catch any man's attention, but what young man would want to keep company with a girl with no manners to speak of? He took all the blame for her behavior, for he treated her more like a son than a daughter.

John Winslow had not a subtle bone in his body. Expressing himself openly and swearing frequently, his eyes would turn black as his temper exploded, often with little provocation. Only in Emily's presence had he, with great effort, restrained himself.

But with Rachel he had been different. He taught her to become one with nature. Her playmates were the squirrels and rabbits and animals of the woodland. She was as familiar with the smell of the earth as she was with her mother's special dishes.

More often, than not, she wore britches and would dress in skirts only when her mother insisted. But once out of Emily's sight, Rachel would reach between her legs, pull up the back hem of her skirt, and tuck it in at the waist. That arrangement was quite unladylike, revealing an indecent length of leg, but produced a covert smile from her father.

Rachel idolized her soft-spoken mother and wanted to emulate her, but it was obvious she was more like her father. And in spite of her mother's gentle admonitions, she was a little untamed, imitating the creatures about her, and her father thoroughly approved.

"But the time for commending her wild behavior is over," he told himself. "If anyone can teach her good manners, Mrs. Templeton can."

Maybe, someday, he could come for her when he was settled elsewhere.

Someday…yes, he felt better thinking of that.

CHAPTER FOUR

RACHEL WAS WAITING IN THE CABIN for John when he returned. He had not bargained for what he found. Her lips pursed when he walked in the door and, suddenly, he saw she was not the same Rachel of last summer with her carefree, abandoned ways. Where was the child he had known? Here before him stood a young girl on the threshold of blossoming maturity and the resolute defense he had braced himself with instantly dispelled.

With hands on her hips and eyes narrowed, "Where have you been all day?" she asked accusingly. "I've been looking for you everywhere."

"This is not going to be easy," John thought.

Picking up a plate, she gestured to the chair. "Well, might as well sit down."

Spoon in hand, she turned to the pot on the crane and said, "I've made fresh stew."

John remained where he was, and she turned and looked curiously at him.

"Well?" she asked.

"Rachel...." As he began, a sense of guilt filled him. "We—we need to talk." Avoiding her stare, he ducked his head and ran his hand through his hair, his fingers lingering on the nape of his neck. His courage was faltering. Better to tell her, point-blank here and now, before he became completely unnerved.

Something was wrong—terribly wrong. Rachel sensed it.

"I'm listening."

"Umm...I—we," he began awkwardly, "you might as well know—we're leaving here," he finished in a gust of breath.

She blinked her eyes and then cocked her head as she pushed back her disheveled hair. Perhaps she did not hear him right.

Laying the plate on the table, "Leaving here?" she echoed. "What do you mean leaving here?"

John hesitated.

"What do you mean leaving here?" she repeated.

He raised his head and gave her a decisive stare, determined now that she would not stop him.

"I've been to town and I've deeded this farm to you with Reverend Templeton as your guardian," he blurted out. "You'll be living with them in Wellington and I'm going to the Kan-tuc-kee land."

As though time had been suspended, she looked at him for several moments with disbelief. Then, realizing the words he had spoken were a reality, a queasiness formed in the pit of her stomach and she thought she would be sick. Living in town with strangers! How could Pa do that to her?

"What? You—you can't be serious!" she finally uttered.

John raised his hand in a dismissive action. "I *am* serious, Rachel. My mind is made up. I've made arrangements with Floyd Thompson to take the livestock." John ran his hand over his face. "I—I can't stay anymore. I've got to leave here...now!"

She was suddenly aghast. This land was all she had known. Memories swiftly sent her back in time. The transformation of this land by her father—building their cabin—springs that came every year with whispered promises of renewed life—summers and their adventures of discovery—autumns with their harvests, winters spent planning for another cycle of seasons and always the soft voice of her mother—gone—all gone. How hard she had worked all winter keeping starvation away! And now Pa was leaving her! Her world—all she'd ever known—was disappearing like the chimney's smoke in the wind.

"But what about me?" she cried stormily, as her hand flattened on her chest. "No!" With a shake of her head and folding of the arms, she turned from him. "I'm staying here. You can't make me go!"

"And just how do you aim to live here alone?" John asked. "Fences need mending and crops to be planted among a thousand other things. Who will take care of you? You certainly can't do it."

Rachel had seen her father in a fit of anger many times. But right now, the anger she felt herself was indescribable. Though her heart had been broken by her mother's death, she had put aside her own grief and had taken care of him, cooked for him, fed him and nursed him without a single "thank you" from him. But she had done it gladly, for he was her family. And now he did not want her anymore and had signed her away to some strangers that she had met only a couple of times!

"Take care of me?" she threw over her shoulder. "I've taken care of things around here all winter without your help and now you say you are leaving here, and I've got to leave, too?"

"That's different," he reasoned. "Sure, I know winter has its share of work, but spring and summer are the hardest months.

"Please try to understand," John said, reaching his hand to clasp her arm. "I'll go crazy if I stay here. I've *got* to get away."

With a cry she wrenched her arm away from him.

John dropped his hand.

"How can you leave here knowing that Mother is buried out back!"

"I'm sorry, Rachel," he apologized.

Whirling back again, she seared him with her look. John shrank back from her.

"Sorry? Sorry?" she uttered. "You don't care about me. You only care about yourself and what *you* want!"

Waving her hand at him, she cried, "Well…well go ahead. See if I care!" Waving her hand at him, she cried, "Running away, are you? Go on. Run! I don't need you—I don't need anybody!"

Turning from him and working furiously about the cabin, Rachel removed her mother's precious china from the table and deposited it on the sideboard. It was apparent her father was not going to eat. The fire had died down in the fireplace and she swung the spider that held the stew back into the hearth. Picking up the pot of tea that was now tepid, she crossed to the door and lifting the latch, stepped out and poured it on her mother's roses. Stepping quickly inside the cabin, she banged the vessel down on the sideboard.

As he remained silent, watching every move she made, Rachel stole a wary look at him.

Finally, she realized he was not going to change his mind. It was set in motion and nothing she could say or do would change the course he had chosen.

"So…you want me to pack now and leave? All right! Don't let me stand in your way! You don't want me around anymore? Well…good riddance to you too!"

Stung by her words, John winced, turned, and dejectedly walked out the door.

"There! I've hurt him!" Rachel thought with satisfaction, watching his retreating back.

"How dare he," she thought, indignantly, "turn me out of my own home!"

Soon her anger lost its edge.

"I'm leaving…I'm leaving," echoed over and over in her mind.

With a passionate sadness catching at her throat, she looked around the cabin and said, "Mother, I don't want to leave you or this place." She fingered her mother's delicate tablecloth as she glanced at the organ in the corner, precious articles that her mother Emily had brought with her from Pennsylvania, things that brought a little civilization to the crude cabin.

Sparse and solitary though it was, it was still home.

Closing her eyes, she could almost hear her mother's melodic voice, teaching her the beloved hymns of the church. Her heart began to constrict as she thought of leaving.

"But…how can I?" cried her heart.

Rachel walked to the window and, drawing back the lace curtain, spotted her mother's grave in front of a grove of oak trees. The spring rains had packed the soil into mud. She wished she had suggested burying Mother in the open land instead of that shady spot. "Grass will have a hard time growing there.

"Who will take care of Mother's grave when I'm gone?" Her

voice broke. "Keep the weeds from overtaking?" She stared at the mound of dirt pondering some way to convince her father to let her stay.

Rachel stood forlornly for a few more moments, remembering small things: the roses and flowers her mother had planted, colorful against the weathered cabin, the row of apple trees leading to the corral and her mother drying bushels of apples for the coming year's pies. Rachel's eyes grew misty and she shivered as the memories' warmth went from her heart.

"Mama," Rachel whispered, "Pa says I have to leave here, but I promise…whatever it takes…or however long it takes…I'll come back. That you can count on. I'll be back."

Reluctantly, she closed the shutters and moved from the window, gathered a few clothes together and tied them up.

With a sinking heart, Rachel took one last look around, drinking in every article in the room.

And each piece of furniture seemed to whisper, "Goodbye! Goodbye!"

She answered softly, "Goodbye," through blinding tears.

John resisted glancing at Rachel as he mounted his horse and lifted her up behind him.

Rachel was tempted to lean her face against his back as tears threatened to spill down her cheeks. She prayed, "Lord, why don't you hear me and help me? Mother said you would not put anything on me that I would not be able to bear…but I don't think I can bear this." It was all she could do to hang onto his waist for she wanted so desperately to slide off the horse and run back home.

All the way to Wellington there was only silence. If only she could understand how he felt. He loved her, he truly did. He just could not cope anymore. She reminded him of Emily too much. The memories were crushing his heart.

Arriving in Wellington, John slowed his horse as though trying to postpone their separation. He knew the church social was taking place today and regretted parting with Rachel in this setting. Reining his horse in front of the church grounds, he dismounted and reached up to help her down.

Glancing at Rachel and noting her expression, he wondered if she would cooperate. His fears were assuaged when she suddenly reached for John's shoulders, allowing him to encircle her waist and set her on the ground. He knotted the reins to the rail and, without a word, turned and walked toward the church as she sullenly followed.

CHAPTER FIVE

IT WAS EIGHT O'CLOCK IN THE MORNING and this second Saturday of May held the promise of blue, cloudless skies. Sunlight streamed into Ransom's bedroom through the white-curtained window as a mockingbird, perched on the birch tree outside, woke him from deep sleep. A smile tugging at his lips, he closed his eyes again. He knew he'd overslept, but the warmth of the sun and sounds of nature summoned him to snuggle a little longer. He draped an arm over his eyes to block out the sun and slumped deeper into the bed.

"Ransom!" his mother called from the foot of the stairs, with a tinge of irritation in her voice, "It's nearly time for breakfast!"

It wasn't like her to call like that, as she lived by the endless rules of etiquette and never knowingly departed from them. If anything, she would have sent Delcey the maid to rap on his door.

His eyes flew open again and fuzzy-mouthed, he called, "Be there in a few minutes, Mother."

Settling back into the familiar sag of his mattress and freeing one leg from under the coverlet, Ransom opted for a few more moments in bed as he stretched his lips with a yawn.

The youngest of the Templeton sons, eighteen-year-old Ransom had grown into a handsome young man, already over six feet tall. Wherever he went, his broad shoulders, wavy, deep auburn hair, and dancing hazel eyes drew furtive glances from young ladies and open appreciation from their mothers, who hoped that Reverend Jacob Templeton's youngest son would favor their daughters with his affection.

His oldest brother Will owned a saw mill and the mill had been practically at a standstill all winter. Except for making furniture and selling a few pieces, they would have had no business at all. But, with the thawing of spring, business became brisk and Ransom had been working hard for several weeks in the mill, so he rewarded himself with extra time in bed. This day would start soon enough.

It was a special day. It was the opening of the social season of the three main churches in town and as his thoughts turned to the dinner on the church grounds at noon, he smiled. The ladies set great store by these functions, which served not only as fellowship with members of other churches, but also provided opportunities for making suitable matches for matrimony.

Ransom's circle of friends included many of the girls of the community, but feeling a strong call to ministry, he avoided any emotional entanglement, much to the dismay of Sally Munsen.

He groaned and turned on his side as she crossed his mind. The one major blot on an otherwise perfect day.

Sally was the apple of her father Wyatt's eye and being thoroughly spoiled, her every whim was quickly satisfied. Sally's pale blond hair, blue eyes and coquettish ways captivated many young men who were constantly at her beck and call hoping to win her affections, but Ransom was indifferent to her. She had pursued Ransom for two years and at times her endless goal of conquest wore thin.

The wealthy and successful Munsen family wielded great influence in the church and though Ransom longed to put her in her place, he was mindful of the trouble it would cause his father in his official capacity as pastor. So, Ransom did his best to ignore her.

He pitied those who fell for her, and one young man in particular...Wade Bennett.

"Ransom!" sounded the second call.

"Right away, Mother," Ransom answered as he leapt from the bed, scrambling to get dressed.

Pouring water into the basin, he washed the sleep from his eyes and peered at the shaving mirror, jutting his chin, turning this way and that as he rubbed the soft stubble on his face.

His older brothers Will and James had completed the university and were now in active ministry with their father in Wellington. Will had recently married and James was engaged with plans to be married in the summer.

"Perhaps today will be the day to tell Father what's on my heart," Ransom remarked aloud to his reflection in the mirror. Frowning, "I just hope he doesn't think my decision to enter ministry is made merely in the spirit of family tradition."

Ransom would be entering the university in the fall and while his friends were distracted by the matters of the day, grooming themselves in their fathers' businesses or farms, for the day when they would take charge, his goals were clear. He would get his degree, marry a suitably decorous girl, and settle down in ministry with his father at Wellington…in that order.

"No hurry to give my heart away," he spoke again. No one could deter him from his intentions. He was secure in his itinerary and looked forward to the fulfillment of his dreams.

No, love and marriage were not for him…at least not for the next few years.

CHAPTER SIX

THE SMELL OF ROASTING MEAT wafted across the church lawn to the community from beef and pork cooked to perfection in deep pits during the night. Tables were spread out over the yard beneath makeshift tents. Benches and chairs, placed in the shadows of the pines and oaks, encouraged pleasant conversation on the events of the day. Men: the price of seed and planting times. The matronly women: childbirth and rearing of children and who was engaged, and who not. Under the watchful eye of these women, young ladies would be escorted by young men on the pretext of exploring the church grounds so familiar to them all.

The church that Jacob Templeton was pastor of was, by far, the largest church in Wellington sitting on several acres. The wide driveway that curved around the front and ended on the east side of the building was full of saddled horses and carriages that began arriving at mid-morning.

The carriage bearing the Munsen family drew rein in the spot allocated for them by the church board as Jacob Templeton came across the lawn to meet them.

"Everyone in the community must be here," said Sally, to no one in particular, as she looked over the grounds swarming with people.

Wade Bennett and his father were arranging seating. Standing with the Pendletons, were her neighbors, the Kennedys and the Reynolds. Henry Taylor was standing with his wife Lydia in conversation with Lee and Eliza Hardin.

Sally did not spot Ransom on the lawn and twisting around in the carriage, frantically searching among the tethered saddle horses, she spied the sorrel he usually rode.

"He's here!" she whispered, shaking with anticipation. Looking across the yard, she saw Mrs. Templeton and stifled the urge to jump unceremoniously from the carriage. Such a breach of etiquette would never do! "It would be just like her to tell Ransom," she muttered under her breath as she fluffed out any wrinkles in her dress, "especially after she caught Wade and me kissing last year!"

Though no gossip circulated after that incident, she sensed Elizabeth kept a watchful eye on her.

Ransom set great store by his mother's opinion and tried to emulate her in matters of etiquette and when around him or his mother, Sally was always on her best behavior.

When she was growing up, Ransom had never seemed very attractive to her. He was just the pastor's young, gangling son. But since that day two years ago, when she returned home from Miss Lillian's Academy in the East, she had cared for him. It was as simple as that.

She had been sitting with her family in their designated pew when he walked into church with his mother on his arm. Even now, she could recall how his hazel eyes lit with recognition when he passed her.

She wanted him, had dreamed about it. Never denied anything by her doting father—anything—whether it was horse or frock or trip to Charleston, she feverishly sought any opportunity to gain his attention. Day after day, when Sally had been in his company, she thought that the very next time he saw her he would propose. But the next time came and went, and nothing happened.

Ransom's reserve tantalized her. It enticed her more than anything her father had ever offered her. Her fear that he would meet someone and become engaged while at university was her worst nightmare and she lay at night scheming ways to gain his attention and affection. In hindsight, she feared her open and direct approaches in the past might have pushed him away. Her tactics would be different today. She would flirt with any boy who gave her the time of day. The opportunities would be numerous as many had already succumbed to her charms.

Ransom's proposal might be hard-won, but win it she would, she told herself determinedly.

Heather Welling came hurrying to the carriage. Giggling, she spoke, "Ransom is here. Lacy Dickson and Eileen Young are with him. If you're going to get his attention, you'd better hurry."

"Hush!" Sally retorted abruptly, looking around to make certain no one had overheard. "Do you want someone to hear you?"

She bit her lip and frowned. "I'll figure out something to do. Surely, I can think of some way to win his heart before this day is over! After all—he's leaving in a few months."

Disembarking the carriage and leaving Heather, Sally strolled throughout the crowd looking for Ransom.

Wade Bennett, catching sight of Sally, hurried across the lawn, and stationed himself by her side, refusing to budge regardless of her attempts to divert him. She groaned inwardly—he was going to be difficult today, she could see that. She had tried to ignore him for the last week and he wasn't having any of it.

Utterly smitten with Sally, Wade had been involved in more than one scuffle when others' attentions to Sally raised his ire. As far as he was concerned, Sally belonged to him and no one else. Meddlesome and dangerous as he was, Sally had become adept at keeping him in hand.

An outsider would have mistaken Wade for Sally's brother. His hair was as blonde as hers, and their features were so similar—the sharp angle of the chin and porcelain pallor of the skin which turned pink without much encouragement from the sun.

And should a stranger linger long enough, their personalities, vindictive and revengeful, would have been the final convincer that they were cut from the same cloth.

"Wade," she said, with her brightest smile, "do be a dear and fetch me a glass of tea. I'm absolutely parched."

Wade eyed her askance. She had avoided him for several days and he was annoyed, but reluctantly did as she requested.

"Finally!" she said to herself with relief as he shuffled away. At his scowling backward glance, she threw him another smile.

"Where is Ransom?" she said under her breath, scanning the crowd. Glimpsing Reverend Templeton talking with her father,

Sally gathered her skirts and walked over, hoping to catch sight of her wished-for young cavalier. Before she had a chance to speak with the Reverend, Elizabeth approached her husband.

"Why, Sally! How pretty you look today!" Elizabeth commented.

"Thank you, Mrs. Templeton. I—"

"Jacob," Elizabeth interrupted, turning to her husband. "Don't you think it's best to offer prayer so the dinner can begin?"

Nodding, he dispersed the young men at hand throughout the scattered crowd, gathering them for the pastor's blessing.

Electing to eat beneath a clump of oak trees with Gerald Miller, who not only owned the town barbershop, but was an avid student of scripture, Ransom spent the afternoon discussing church doctrine. Sally sat within earshot with Wade firmly entrenched beside her. She wanted Ransom's attention and though irritated by Wade's persistence, she laughed gaily when he complimented her. But as her voice rose ever higher in frivolity, she saw that Ransom took no notice of her.

"I agree with you Brother Miller, as Abraham was justified by faith, so are we. As Abraham was before the law, we being the branch grafted in, are also the seed of Abraham for we walk by faith also."

Sally sniffed. "Scripture! That's where his attention is! Me in my finest frock and he doesn't even glance my way! Surely, he can see I am the prettiest girl here. But I won't give up—no—not Sally Munsen!"

CHAPTER SEVEN

AS THE AFTERNOON WORE ON, the laughter and talking became less lively and children nodded to sleep in the arms of parents as the stillness of late day began to descend upon the crowd.

Suddenly, a tall man appeared, gaunt and wearing clothes that were too large and looking somewhat disarrayed.

"Is Reverend Templeton here?" he asked a circle of men.

One of the men rose and said, "I'll fetch him."

A girl, not quite a woman, stood close behind him. She was not much more than five feet, three inches tall and his tall frame overshadowed her.

Fans stopped in mid-swish and a ripple of murmuring ran through the crowd, wondering who the strangers were. He was certainly not a member of any church congregation they knew. "Who are they?" "I've never seen them before." "Oh, yes," someone remembered. "He lives on a farm outside of Wellington—they keep to themselves. Think his name is Winslow—heard his wife died a few months ago."

Ransom, who had been engrossed in conversation with Gerald Miller, heard this exchange, and turned in the direction of the strangers.

There stood the prettiest girl he had ever encountered. Cascading down the girl's shoulders was thick black hair as dark as a raven's wing and wild as the river on the edge of town when spring rains caused it to overflow its banks.

Though many of those assembled were looking their way, Rachel sensed his eyes upon her and she turned and looked at Ransom with defiant dark eyes. Intrigued, Ransom stared. He could not help himself though his mother's past admonition to refrain from such behavior clanged in his mind.

She straightened her back and stood proud. Brushing the hair out of her face with the back of her hand, she refused to look away, her look daring some insolent remark from him. Never, in all his eighteen years, had he seen such outright impertinence from any girl before.

But...there was something about her.

Fascinated and unconsciously edging forward, he searched her eyes, his own asking unspoken questions, “What is it? What’s wrong?”

He held her gaze and wondered with amazement how anyone could emit so much emotion without saying a single word.

At his silent inquisition, her eyes began to tear and the defiance in them slipped away, leaving only raw, aching hurt.

A feeling such as he had never felt before overwhelmed him. He was mesmerized and his pulse quickened. He tried to look away but found he could not. The feeling that his life was about to dramatically change pressed heavily upon him.

As the man in front of her reached back and tugged on her arm, the girl’s eyes unwillingly left Ransom’s as Pastor Templeton and Elizabeth ushered the two of them away from the crowd and toward the church.

Ransom gazed at her retreating back as she was pulled away and concluded that she was no flirtatious, simple-minded girl. There was a certain wildness and earthiness about her that was absent in every other young woman present.

He finally noticed the girl’s well-worn and shabby dress, a stark comparison to the silks and fine muslin that graced the women of the community. She was so different from everyone else.

And those eyes….

The silent exchange between Ransom and the scruffy girl had not escaped Sally. His look was what she had longed to see in his eyes for her but had never. A pain slashed at her heart and there were hurt and bewilderment in her face.

Wade peered at her stricken expression and clenched his jaw. Fumbling clumsily to grasp her hand, she brushed it away as she rose from her seat and stared at Ransom. She had thought she could make him love her. Tried in every way she could imagine. But for the first time in her pampered life, she faced the fact that perhaps she would not get her way.

As Ransom stood watching the disappearing girl, Sally clenched her hands in the soft fullness of her dress.

With the aid of two servants that morning, it had taken two hours before Sally was satisfied with her appearance. Her hair had been arranged high at the back of her head with golden curls falling to her shoulders…all with Ransom in mind. And now…it was not her that he wanted at all, but that disheveled, backwoods creature!

Sally nearly stomped her foot at the injustice of it all. His lack of attention was frustrating enough…but his open admiration of someone so unsophisticated and primitive was maddening. She wanted to cry.

Her nails dug into her palms as the urge to protect her dream of matrimony to Ransom consumed her. Sally did not know who this girl was or where she came from, but if there was a chance to discredit her, she would.

Feeling Wade's hand on her arm, Sally dropped her head, looked intently at his expectant face staring up at her and thought, "I'll use anyone to make my dreams come true…even him."

CHAPTER EIGHT

JACOB WALKED BEHIND THE DESK and motioned for John to sit down. "What can I do for you, Mr. Winslow? Please have a seat."

John Winslow removed his hat.

"Begging your pardon, Parson, I'd rather not. Can't stay." He fingered the edge of the slouch hat in his hand and lowered his head.

He cleared his throat, then looked up and said, "I know you met my daughter Rachel when my wife died."

Jacob nodded.

John paused for a moment and then rushed on. "I'm asking you to take Rachel as your ward."

Winslow shifted his stance and turned away from Rachel, shutting out any pleas she might voice. But there was no need for him to do so for she refused to look at him. As she stared at the bare wooden floor, every word her father spoke sent a dart into her heart.

"She's fifteen now, almost sixteen," he continued. Looking at Pastor Templeton, his tone grew soft and a trace of pleading could be heard in this tall, proud man's voice.

"She'll work hard and earn her keep. She needs religion like her mother had. She can read some and she is smart. Heard of the Kan-tuc-kee land and that's where I'm bound. I won't be taking her with me though. Too dangerous, not much settlement, and—well—I hear there's Indians."

Reaching into his coat, John extracted the legal documents that he had carefully hidden from Rachel. With a sudden motion he thrust the papers at Jacob.

He drew a ragged breath and said, "I've deeded my farm over to her as she is my only kin. Attorney Adkins drew up all the paperwork. I've made you her guardian and trustee of the farm. She can't work the farm by herself now, but it's there for her when she gets married."

After a quick stroke of his beard, he said, "Uh…I—I'll be going now."

Rachel balled her fists and had a sudden desire to clutch his coat and cry, "Don't leave me, Pa!" but despair repressed it.

Then John Winslow put on his hat and walked out the door, without a glance or word to his daughter.

Rachel winced as the door banged shut. For as long as she would live, she would never forget that sound, the sound that would haunt her in days to come—the sound of desertion as he closed her out of his life. He was gone! The man she cared for more than life itself! Abandoned, as though she were nothing more to him than a worn-out piece of fabric!

Rachel had been stunned on the ride to town. This couldn't really be happening, not to her. All her cherished memories were of Mother and Pa. Strangers in her mind were outsiders…foreigners. Now, because of her father's decision, they were interloping into her serene world. She could not—would not—surrender to them and their ways!

She had seen their looks when she arrived. They were not the looks of welcome. She was proud of who she was and vowed no one would change her!

Jacob and Elizabeth were speechless. The girl standing in front of them with her head slightly bent had just been made their ward. The chance to protest never arose as John Winslow disappeared as quickly as he had come.

Sitting down behind the desk, Jacob silently read the documents. Handing them to Elizabeth and looking up, he observed Rachel standing by the door, poised, as though ready to take flight.

He rose and motioned toward a chair and said softly, "There, sit down, child."

Rachel refused to lift her head as without warning tears stung her eyes. Her trembling mouth tried to set itself in martial lines but failed.

Jacob walked cautiously from behind the desk and pulled out the chair for her. “Please…sit down, Rachel,” he asked.

Rachel did not want to sit down. Instead, still hoping Pa had changed his mind, she wanted to cross to the closed door, open it and run from the room into the arms of her father.

Trying to control the tears that lingered on her lower lids, she stood still for a few moments, daring not to blink lest they slip down her cheeks. Then, she wiped the back of her hand across her eyes, reluctantly crossed to the chair and sat down, clutching the dun-colored parcel to her chest. In her haste, she had brought nothing but the very basics of clothing. Not even her mother’s daguerreotype.

Jacob put his hand under Elizabeth’s elbow, guiding her toward the sanctuary.

“We’ll be back in a few moments, Rachel,” said Jacob.

Rachel cocked her head and watched them from the corner of her eye until they were out of sight.

“My—my!” Elizabeth exhaled, “Jacob, what are we going to do? We have never been guardian of someone else’s child before and we know nothing about this girl. What kind of father would abandon his child on a stranger’s doorstep and leave without saying a word to his own daughter? Not so much as a fare-thee-well!”

“I know, I know,” Jacob answered absently as he patted her arm.

“With all our responsibilities, it will be difficult to raise this girl,” Elizabeth mused. “She would have to be educated and learn the social graces our congregation expects. These people have been staunch members of our church for years and I’m afraid she might not fit in.”

In the past Jacob had encountered all manner of responsibility that came with ministry, but nothing like this. Should he shirk this request under the pretense of his own hectic schedule? Should he search for another church family willing to take this girl in? Her appearance indicated she was totally different from the members of his church. There was a definite wildness about her, something almost uncivilized. Elizabeth was right. The members might not readily accept someone like her.

But the deed was done. Legal and binding.

And for what end did God call him? Whatever background and station in life she had come from, Christ called all to come unto him. *Whosoever will let him come.* Jacob presently came to the conclusion that God must have a foreordained plan that eluded him at the moment. Didn't Christ tell his disciples that he had other sheep they knew not of? He had learned the ways of God are often strange to mankind, not always discernible at the present.

With a sense of resolution, he knew what they must do.

"But is it about fitting in, Elizabeth? Shouldn't we care for those less fortunate than ourselves? What would Christ say? Have we evolved into just a church of social graces? What of Matthew 25:35 which says: 'I was an hungered, and ye gave me meat: I was thirsty, and ye gave me drink: I was a stranger, and ye took me in.' Can we ignore Christian charity? I know much of the load will be on you, dear. I can help with scripture and Ransom can help with her studies until he leaves for the university. But with her mother dead only a short while, she will need a woman's care."

Elizabeth sighed. "Yes, I suppose you're right. But she may not be ready for my mothering. Just losing her mother and now her father will take some time to heal."

He smiled at her and put his arm around her shoulders. "I'm sure she'll eventually come around.

CHAPTER NINE

RACHEL SOAKED LUXURIOUSLY in a hot bath that evening after Delcey delivered a light supper to her room. How enjoyable the water was and how good it felt to be waited on. She relaxed and after a time, her predicament did not seem nearly as dreadful.

"Thank goodness, I wasn't asked to eat in the dining room with the others!" she thought as she sat in the lilac-scented water. Her nerves were on edge when she had arrived and though she hadn't eaten since breakfast, Rachel didn't think she could swallow a single bite in front of them—at least not tonight.

Hearing a ruckus in the street, Rachel climbed from the tub and dressed in her nightgown.

Forgetting her dilemma for the moment, Rachel sat in the window of her upstairs bedroom and watched people milling about the street. Everyone seemed in a hurry—unlike quiet moonlit nights spent on the farm.

Rachel smiled, remembering the warm evenings her family sat outdoors watching the rising moon while she chased fireflies. And after catching them, she presented the blinking insects as small trophies to her admiring parents.

The curtains fluttered as the wind picked up, carrying a smell of rain in the air. Rachel closed her eyes and lifted her chin, feeling the cool breeze that swept back her hair. A light drizzle began to fall, and the streets quickly emptied, leaving Rachel with nothing to stare at, except soft lights emanating from the windows.

Sighing, Rachel pulled the window shut and closed the shutters.

She wandered about the room examining the furnishings. The splendor of the house was unlike anything she had ever known. So many rooms! There were rooms for sitting, for eating, and for sleeping. Rooms filled with exquisite furniture. "Some imported," Elizabeth had said when showing her about the home. And the fine china on the silver supper tray! By comparison, only a few pieces of porcelain tableware remained at the farm as most of them had been broken through the years and replaced with pewter.

Running her hand over the bed's coverlet, Rachel pressed lightly on the mattress. How large the bed was! And how high! It was nothing like her bedtick filled with straw and pine needles.

Climbing the steps by the bed and lying down, she sank into softness that was softer than the bear skin that Pa had used to cover her bedtick. A giggle escaped her lips and she laughed aloud at her own silliness.

"So…this is how other people live!" she remarked to the ceiling.

A clap of thunder and a flash of lightning caught her attention and she glanced toward the window thinking of the farm. "Did Mr. Thompson get the livestock?" she worried. "Pa never mentioned the ducks and chickens. I wonder…did he take those, too?"

"You're making a new beginning," Mrs. Templeton had explained to Rachel that afternoon when she had fretted about leaving the farm. "Life is about beginnings and endings. Just as each day begins and ends."

New beginning? Out of all the words Mrs. Templeton said to her, those were the most frightening. That would mean turning her back on all that she knew.

Turning over on her stomach and laying her head on her arms, she mulled over the fact that she had been thrust into a situation that she could do nothing about. She couldn't have control over her own property, much less control over herself. These people did not know her—thought she was some helpless child—but she had taken care of Pa, and she could take care of herself, too. "I'm nearly grown." she thought. "Maybe the time will pass quick enough and I can go back home." She felt a little better at that.

"But how can I live in this town?" she lamented. Already, she missed the farm with its familiar sights and sounds, the hawk with its shrill call, the sight of raccoon, squirrel, and deer, the fields with their crops and the smell of the earth.

"How can I stay here, in this house?"

She belonged at the farm and she determined that she would get back to those rich, fertile acres. Somehow, she would get back to Mother. After all—she did promise her.

With a strength that seemed to rally in times of distress, she thought, "Well, make the best of it, Rachel, girl. Just remember, you won't be here forever. Things will eventually change for you and you can go back home."

But an uneasy feeling was gnawing at her. She had been forced into a world she would never have chosen. Gone was the simple and uncomplicated life she had before Mother died. Something in her seemed to echo, "Watch out! Watch out!" And with a shudder, she rolled over and climbed under the coverlet.

CHAPTER TEN

THE NEXT MORNING, RACHEL WAS ROUSED FROM SLEEP by a knock on the door.

Stirring, with a sense of dread, she thought, dulled with sleep, "What was I worrying about last night when I went to bed?"

She finally opened her eyes and as the cobwebs fell away, remembered that she was not home.

Another knock sounded and without waiting for an invitation, Elizabeth opened the door and waltzed into the room.

"Good morning, Rachel," she nearly sang the words as she pulled back the curtains. "It's Sunday. We have church service today and you will be going with us."

Church service? Rachel never attended one but, from her Mother's description of such goings on, her interest was piqued.

"Pastor Templeton made a good speech over Mother's grave," she pondered, "and if that's what it's going to be like, it might not be so bad."

However, being confined in one room with so many strangers was another thing entirely and made her heart speed up as she cringed and thought about hiding somewhere.

"I know it is early," said Elizabeth, "but I must look over the clothes you brought with you."

She added, "I've asked James—he's our second son—to take a message to my oldest son William and his wife Jane"

Elizabeth glanced at Rachel, mentally assessing her figure.

"Jane is about your size and I've asked her to send over a couple of dresses until we can outfit you this week. We will go to Langdron's Store and pick out some nice material for you. Won't that be grand?"

Grand? Grand would be on the farm with Pa.

Rachel did not answer while her eyes warily followed Elizabeth's every move.

As Elizabeth rambled on, there was another knock on the door.

Elizabeth crossed the room and opened the door. "Oh, good! They've come. Thank you, Delcey."

She turned, holding packages in her arms and with the excitement of a child, unceremoniously plopped them on the bed.

Elizabeth tore into them excitedly and suddenly with a grin on her face, she paused, turned to Rachel and said with slight embarrassment, "I know you must think I'm silly, Rachel, but I just love packages and presents even if they're not mine."

Turning her attention back to the packages, she lifted a dress in the air and shook it out, examining the embroidered detail. "Look at this dress!" she exclaimed. "Blue as wild lupine! Oh, Rachel, you will look just divine!" Elizabeth said addressing the garment more than Rachel.

Elizabeth had only sons…no daughters. She had always wanted a daughter and she imagined, for a brief moment, the delight of taking this wild creature and transforming her from a woodland nymph into a social debutante. It was a heady feeling and lost in thought, a soft smile on her lips, she laid the dress carefully on the foot of the bed, gently smoothing out imaginary wrinkles.

Suddenly remembering that it was Sunday, Elizabeth straightened and said briskly, "Well! That's that!"

She headed for the door, but then looked back. "If you will get dressed, my dear, I'll come back and do your hair," she said. Happy as if it were Christmas morning, Elizabeth gave Rachel a beaming smile and then left the room.

Rachel frowned at her retreating back.

I don't want to feel divine. I want to wake up in my own bed in my own home.

From beneath the coverlet her feet kicked at the opened packages.

I don't want this dress and these doo-dads.

Sent with the dresses were the necessary undergarments and even a pair of shoes. After several minutes, half-heartedly resigning herself to the situation she was in, Rachel eyed the fashionable clothes with curiosity.

Hesitantly, she swung her legs over the side of the bed and tried a slipper on. It was a little large, but she could make do.

Fingering the silk dress, she said aloud, "Such clothes!" Never had she owned such nice things.

The sound of fussing blue jays drew her attention to the window and the finery was instantly forgotten. Dropping the dress, she crossed the room and opened the shutters. Swinging the window open wide, she leaned her elbows on the windowsill as she peered outside, drinking in the scent of roses and honeysuckle drifting up from the flower beds in the front yard.

It was Sunday and the shops were closed. Only a few people were out and about. Deserted streets would soon come alive as horses and carriages transported parishioners to church.

Disappointment swelled within her as she looked out at the upper stories of tall buildings, rather than freshly plowed fields ready for spring planting. The cloudless sky radiated a silvery blue as the morning sun kissed the hills beyond the perimeter of the town. She felt captive in her room and sighing she turned back to the task at hand.

She was clumsily hooking up the last hooks of her dress when she was interrupted again by a knock.

"May I come in, Rachel?" Elizabeth called.

Glancing toward the door, she answered, "Yes."

Elizabeth swooped into the room and laying her hand on her chest, exclaimed, "Oh, Rachel, you look splendid! That dress compliments your beautiful dark eyes."

Placing a small basket that she was carrying on the table, Elizabeth crossed to stand behind her and finished hooking up the dress.

Placing hands on Rachel's shoulders, she said, "Now...if you will go and sit at the mirror, I will do your hair. I thought we might do something simple, nothing complicated. You have such beautiful hair, so thick and black."

She pulled the chair out for Rachel and motioned for her to sit. "You know some girls have to spend hours in their toilette to look pretty, but you have such a natural beauty."

Elizabeth reached into the basket and said, "I've brought some of my egrettes. These, my dear, are pins that can be fastened to a dress or the hair."

Holding a blue egrette to Rachel's hair, she said, "Yes…I think they would look nice in your dark hair and…."

Talking incessantly, Elizabeth began to brush Rachel's hair with long, gentle strokes and sweeping the sides up, fastened them with ornate egrettes.

A warm feeling stole over Rachel as she remembered her own mother brushing her hair and she relaxed momentarily in that sweet memory.

Elizabeth's enthusiasm was sweeping Rachel into the magic of the moment and though she tried to guard herself against any show of approval, she found herself melting under Elizabeth's sweet friendliness.

She was being pampered and cared about. And in this enchanting instant, the stress and hardships of the last several months seemed to be fading away.

Part of her wanted to relax and bathe in the promise of a new life without the cares that had weighed her down and the other part wanted to flee this town.

Like a rain-swollen river sweeping everything in its path, she felt powerless to stop the flow of this turn of events.

Wistfully, she thought, "Truly, I've had some bad times. But this must be the due season Mother spoke about. What was that scripture? Oh, yes…*Be not weary in well doing, for in due season you shall reap if you faint not.*"

She had been weary, all right. Bone weary.

Elizabeth placed hands on Rachel's shoulders again as they both peered in the mirror. "There! Oh, how beautiful you are, Rachel!"

As though Rachel was a trophy to be admired, Elizabeth proudly said, "I can't wait for the others to see you!"

CHAPTER ELEVEN

AS RACHEL ENTERED THE DINING ROOM, Ransom looked up and a small catch caught his breath. He did not think it possible she could have become more beautiful than yesterday. A single glance took in everything about her from her tanned skin to the dress she was wearing.

The attraction Ransom felt had him bewildered. What was happening here? As she took her seat at the table, he looked away, confused.

He always felt the type of girl he would court and eventually marry would be prudent, proper, above reproach and acceptable to society, indeed, complimentary to the calling he was contemplating.

Looking into his coffee cup with disgust, he wanted to shake himself. "Why on earth am I thinking about courting and marriage?"

Last night, he had discovered that Rachel was to be a ward of his household and his anxiety increased when he found he had been chosen to attend to her studies over the summer.

Just being near her was enough to make his head giddy, and now she would be living under the same roof!

Somehow…just somehow, he had to find a way to keep his distance from her! He considered talking to his father, but no plausible excuse came to mind. And should anyone discover his struggle, it would be too embarrassing to explain.

"No," he decided firmly, "better to keep my feelings a secret."

He determined that this young woman would not come between him and his plans of the future.

And yet, sitting here with her, it took great effort to keep his eyes from straying to her face, hoping for a glimpse into her dark eyes.

"You're quiet this morning, son," remarked Jacob as Delcey refilled his cup with coffee.

Ransom shrugged a shoulder and dared a look at Rachel out of the corner of his eye. "Just things on my mind, Father," and went back to eating.

He brought his head up at the sound of a sharp intake of breath from his mother.

Rachel, unknowingly, was breaking nearly every rule of table etiquette.

Aghast, Elizabeth opened her mouth to address Rachel's table manners, but Jacob laid his hand on her hand and silently shook his head no. There would be time for instruction in manners later.

"I can't let this go on," Elizabeth agonized in thought, drawing her hand from Jacob's. "What would others say? Dear! Dear! William and Jane are coming for dinner today. Knowing Jane as I do, she will point out Rachel's behavior and hurt her feelings. I love Jane a great deal, but she can be rather blunt at times."

Putting her finger to her temple, she thought, "Where did I put that handbook about manners?" Picking up her fork, "I'll search for it before church."

Ransom smothered a grin with the back of his hand.

He finished his coffee and stood up.

"I'll go on ahead to the church this morning," Ransom announced, "if that's all right."

Leaving the table, Ransom made his hasty farewell with an excuse that did not seem plausible, even to him, and was gone.

Jacob raised his eyebrows at Ransom's swift departure. He thought his son was acting strangely and seemed less talkative than usual and hoped it had nothing to do with Rachel. When he broke the news to Ransom that Rachel would be living with them and that he was expected to help with her studies, Ransom seemed less than thrilled.

"Maybe he feels imposed upon, for he certainly did not speak to the girl this morning and did not invite her to join the youth today. Well," Jacob thought with a sigh. "I suppose it will take care of itself in time."

After breakfast, Elizabeth walked into Rachel's room with the book.

"My dear," Elizabeth said with a determined look on her face and pointing to the book in her hand, "I have something I want you to read before church. It might help you understand the custom of our table manners."

She paused as the thought occurred to her that perhaps Rachel could not read well enough. After all, she had been raised in almost total seclusion.

Tentatively, she asked, "You can read, can't you, Rachel?"

Dismissing the thought and patting Rachel on the hand, "Well, never mind," she said. "Read what you can and what you don't understand, feel free to ask. I just *know* you'll conform very easily to these rules. Of course, a couple will not apply since you are a young lady now."

Puzzled, Rachel took the book.

Looking over her shoulder as she left, Elizabeth commented, "We'll be leaving in about thirty minutes."

Rachel ran her finger slowly over the inscription on the cover.

The School of Manners, published in London, 1701.

She opened to the section regarding table manners Elizabeth had marked for her. Scanning it, she read:

- *Never sit down at the table till asked, and after the blessing.*
- *Ask for nothing; tarry till it be offered thee.*
- *Speak not.*
- *Sing not, hum not, wriggle not.*
- *Bite not thy bread but break it.*
- *Take not salt with a greasy knife.*
- *Dip not the meat in the same (the salt).*
- *Look not earnestly at any other that is eating.*
- *Spit not, cough not, nor blow thy nose at table if it may be avoided; but if there be necessity, do it aside, and without much notice.*
- *Lean not thy elbow on the table, or on the back of thy chair.*

- *Stuff not thy mouth so as to fill thy cheeks; be content with smaller mouthfuls.*
- *Blow not thy meat, but with patience wait till it be cool.*
- *Eat not too fast nor with greedy behavior.*
- *Eat not vastly but moderately.*
- *Make not noise with thy tongue, mouth, lips, or breath in thy eating and drinking.*
- *Smell not of thy meat; nor put it to thy nose; turn it not to the other side upward on thy plate.*
- *When moderately satisfied, leave the table.*

"Well! I guess I broke just about every rule there is!" she thought in horror. "They must think—well, it's no telling what they think!"

Pa never cared how she ate and thoroughly enjoyed her lack of restraint. Mother: though she never actually approved of her ways, usually overlooked just about anything she did.

Rachel threw the book down on the bed and gave a short, loud huff. Bad enough she was stuck living here in town, but to become pretentious was enough to turn her stomach.

"I can't fit in with these people!" she exclaimed as she folded her arms across her chest. "If I kept all of these rules it wouldn't do much good to eat, for thinking about every move I made would surely bother my digestion!"

CHAPTER TWELVE

"WHEW!" RANSOM SAID AS HE BLEW OUT HIS BREATH. "I sure acted fey in there this morning! I've got to get hold of myself!"

Mounting his horse and slapping the stirrups, he decided on a short ride in the country to clear his mind before service.

Galloping through town, he passed the Munsen family in their carriage. Recognizing Ransom, Sally gave him a wave. He did not return her greeting.

After passing the last building, which housed the livery, he slowed his sorrel to a walk.

Turning off the main road, he traveled a well-worn path leading through a thicket of woods to the river that was, not only the best place to fish, but the church's baptizing spot.

The river was up from a recent rain and he sat astride his horse a moment watching the swell of the water dash against the shoreline.

Slowly alighting from his horse and breaking a twig, which he promptly placed between his teeth, he absent-mindedly walked toward the water's edge. He leaned his shoulder against one of the huge rocks which dotted that section of the river.

For a long time, Ransom gazed at the water, watching the flow with its hypnotic predictability going only in one direction. You knew where it was heading and where it would blend with other waters. Yes, predictable, even when it overflowed its banks—still in one foreseeable direction.

Rachel coming into his world was not something he had counted on. He had avoided emotional entanglements with the opposite sex all his life. Yet now, uninvited, this girl came stealing in like a thief, threatening his peace of mind. He certainly did not want to feel involved. Not at this point in life.

Overnight, life became unsettling…his head and his emotions

torn in two directions. 'Reliable Ransom', that is what folks said about him. Feet on the ground, knowing where he was going.

"If they could see me now!" he laughed bitterly.

He took the twig from his teeth and threw it into the water where it was quickly carried away by the current. He would not be swayed by her. She was absolutely not the type of girl that fit into his plans and when he did give his heart away, it would be to someone familiar with the church...educated, refined, someone who would be a suitable minister's wife...an asset to him!

This backwoods girl had come into his life and he was not ready for her. When Jacob Templeton told him of his responsibilities to this girl last night, he had started to state flatly and loudly that, under no circumstances, would he take part in her education.

But the look on his father's expectant face caused his protests to rapidly dwindle.

Turning his back to the rock and sliding to the ground, Ransom clasped his arms around his knees, and prayed, "God, I've wanted my whole life to please and serve you."

After much thought, Ransom concluded that he was to mentor the girl. "Ah—that must be it! Sure! That has to be it! She has no family now and God has put me into her life as a substitute family."

Feeling somewhat mollified, he placed a hand against the rock and pushed himself up.

Believing he had received an answer, Ransom walked back to his horse with a lighter heart, mounted, and reaching the main road, turned toward town.

Church had already commenced when Ransom walked in and took his place beside his mother.

As the choir led the congregation in songs from the hymnbook, Ransom and Elizabeth were surprised to hear the sweet musical lilt of Rachel's voice. Truly she had a gift to sing! Elizabeth immediately courted the idea of speaking to Roger Earnhardt about Rachel. He was the director of music and with his training she would become an asset to that department.

CHAPTER THIRTEEN

RANSOM ELECTED TO SPARE RACHEL this first day with the church youth. With her recent separation from her father, he didn't feel she was ready to engage them yet and he told Jacob so.

The youth made plans to meet at the Munsen farm. The carriages began arriving and soon young people were spilling all over the lawn. Ransom was riding his sorrel, and before he dismounted, several young men peppered him with questions.

"You were late for service this morning," Lyle Garrison said.

"Yeah, what happened to you, Ransom?" chimed Jim Richards. "Thought you'd be the first there like usual."

Ransom laughed. "Hey, men!" Dismounting his horse and tying the reins to the rail by the mounting block, he glanced at them sideways and retorted, "I just wanted to be alone and have a talk with God this morning, so I went for a ride. I didn't *intend* to be so late."

"It wouldn't have anything to do with that pretty girl come to live with you, would it, Ransom?" That statement drew smirks from the others.

Ransom nearly winced but he answered lightheartedly. "Say, what's with you fellows?"

"We saw the way you looked at her yesterday." The rest murmured in agreement.

Ransom shifted his stance. "She's pretty, all right," he admitted. "You can see that for yourselves. But listen, don't harass this girl," he warned. "She's different from the others and not used to being around many people. So, go easy and be nice to her."

"Aw, Ransom. You know we're not like that."

With a sudden grin and rolling his eyes, he said, "Sure, sure. Just watch it!"

Sally had watched for an opportunity to get Ransom alone all afternoon. Wade left early to help his father and she was free at last. Finally! Her chance! He was sitting alone in the arbor drinking a glass of cider.

"Hello, Ransom."

"Oh…hello, Sally," he answered, a mite unenthusiastically than she wanted to hear.

"Have you been avoiding me today, Ransom?" she asked. "When you passed our carriage this morning you didn't even return my wave."

"Sorry, Sally. I didn't see you," Ransom said. "I've had things on my mind lately."

"Could it be your new houseguest?"

Unprepared for her candid question, Ransom winced slightly at her words, as if she had touched his inward struggle.

Sally immediately wished she could take back the words at the look on Ransom's face. To accuse Ransom of such a thing would make her look jealous in his eyes. She would not be brought so low. She had learned better than that at the academy.

With a touch of acrimony, he replied, "Sally, this girl needs a home, and needs friends, also. Her mother died recently, and her father deserted her, so she is now alone."

"Oh, I agree with you totally, Ransom," she agreed, changing her tack. "We're supposed to help the poor and underprivileged, even the ignorant ones such as her."

He gave her a skeptical look.

"You and I have so much in common," she cajoled. "We've known the same people and have the same goals."

"I'm not sure what your goals are, Sally, but mine are to enter the university this fall, become degreed, and return to help Father in ministry. This is foremost in my mind and what I intend to accomplish."

"I didn't know you were going to enter the ministry," she said, surprised. "Your father never said a word about it."

He'd said too much.

"He doesn't know—yet."

A minister's wife, she thought. *Reverend Ransom Templeton. Reverend Ransom and Sally Templeton.*

"I'd rather you didn't tell anyone just yet, Sally."

"Oh, you can count on me, Ransom. But if you're going to be a minister, don't you think it's best if you keep your distance from that girl? If you didn't know, there have been rumors circulating."

My rumors.

His lips parted in astonishment. "Rumors? About what?"

"About you and that girl."

"Nonsense," he scoffed. "I just met her yesterday."

"Well…there is," she stated as she twiddled her fingers, "I thought I'd let you know."

Ransom huffed in disgust. "It so happens to be my lot, Sally, that Rachel is staying under my roof. If I can help her in any way, I intend to. It's my Christian duty and that's all there is to it. So, please, don't question me about this anymore."

Sally straightened as if slapped and was tempted to grasp Ransom's arm to win him back from his obvious disapproval, but dared not.

Instead, she replied, "Oh, Ransom, don't misunderstand me. I only want the best for you. We've grown up together and I care about you a great deal. You're more than a friend, you're like a mentor to me and I cherish your friendship very much. Please, don't be mad."

Ransom shrugged. "I'm not mad, Sally. But I'm not engaged to anyone and answer to no one but my superiors and God. I think it's best if we put this aside and don't discuss it anymore."

"All right, Ransom," she answered, her meek tone belying the treacherous thoughts in her mind. She was used to getting her way and she was not quitting and the set expression on her uplifted face warned Ransom that she had not given up.

The mood of day suddenly turned sour and Ransom wanted only to leave and head toward home.

He stood up suddenly, casting a long shadow.

Expressing his goodbyes to his host and hostess, he rode out alone.

CHAPTER FOURTEEN

ARRIVING IN TOWN, Ransom saw the livery stable door open and caught a glimpse of the owner Gus. He liked Gus.

An easygoing older man, Gus had seen his share of trouble. His wife, Christine, had run off with a chapman several years ago and he had turned bitter for quite some time. But becoming a Christian had changed him and he faced each day with renewed hope that she would return.

The townsfolk had their doubts and thought what he was praying about was a foolish impossibility—but Gus still retained his faith that she would come back.

A bay and strawberry roan were tethered to the rail and Ransom reined his horse beside them.

"Hi, yah, Gus," Ransom called through the door as he stepped off the saddle.

Gus was seated on a stool and looked up from the bridle he was mending. "Hello, Ransom," he answered, his face lighting with a smile.

Ransom tied his horse to the railing, stepped inside the shadowy stable lit by a single lantern and seated himself on a bale of hay opposite Gus.

Focused again on the bridle in his hands, Gus mentioned, "I heard you went to the Munsens' today. Did you have a good time?"

"Yeah, I guess," Ransom replied, a touch of irony in his voice.

Looking up, "You guess?" Gus asked. "What's wrong?"

Good old Gus. Nothing much escaped him. As Ransom debated just how much he should divulge, Gus cut into his thoughts.

"Go ahead, Ransom. You know you can tell me anything. I'll pray over whatever is bothering you."

He bent his head to the bridle again as though to give Ransom some privacy.

"Gus, I have a problem. You know Rachel Winslow, the new girl at church this morning that sat next to Mother?"

Gus nodded.

"Well, her mother died a few months ago, and her father decided to go to Kentucky, leaving Rachel behind. She's been made a ward of Father and is living with us."

"Sure," said Gus with a shake of his head. "I'd heard something about that."

"My problem is—" Ransom hesitated. He and Gus talked about a lot of things. Horses, church, price of lumber, man-talk. It was one thing to chew the fat, quite another to discuss something this personal.

"Gus, can I trust you to keep quiet on this?"

"You've got my solemn word on it, Ransom," Gus assured him, raised his head, and gave him a level look beneath his bushy eyebrows. "This is between me, you, and God."

Relaxing, Ransom continued. "I just met her yesterday, but I—I feel these feelings."

Gus urged, "Go on."

"Well—for the first time in my life I feel genuinely attracted to a girl. You know I've always guarded against that sort of thing." Ransom thought back to when he first saw her yesterday and decided he must sound ridiculous.

Rushing on, trying to convince himself more than Gus, "I don't know *what* I feel, but I know it's not love."

Reaching for his pipe and tobacco, Gus dumped the old ashes, filled the pipe, and lit it.

He was very quiet. For a few moments he smoked, and then he asked, "How do you know it's not love, Ransom? I saw the way you looked at the girl at the picnic yesterday."

Giving a trace of a smile, he added, "Seems to me you were pretty taken with her.

"There is such a thing as love at first sight," Gus said confidently.

Ransom frowned. “I don’t know about that,” he commented doubtfully. “I just know it’s not love. Though I’ve never been in love before, I know love must somehow be deeper than just physical attraction.

“You’ve been—you’re—in love with your wife Christine. Can you tell me what it’s like?”

With a ghost of a smile on his lips, Gus thought for a while. “Well, when you see that certain girl your heart just kind of soars. When you’re with her, there’s nothing or nobody else in the whole world but her.”

“What is love?” Gus continued, “I guess that’s a little hard to define. For me, it’s a whole lot about feeling *and* doing.”

He gave a wave with his pipe. “Oh, I know what the townsfolk say about me; they say I’m living in a dream world. But, you know, I still love her and when—and I say when—she walks back through that door, I’m ready to totally forgive. For you see, son, love is not just an emotion, but love is doing.

“Yes, sir,” he affirmed with a nod of his head, “she’s coming back, and we’ll have our scars, but it’ll be better than ever.”

As Gus droned on reminiscing, Ransom totally dismissed the idea of ‘love at first sight’. Such a thought was alien to his way of thinking.

Yes, he felt a great attraction to Rachel, but that’s all it was, just an attraction. He would not allow himself to believe otherwise. She just did not fit into his scheme of things.

He would be only a mentor to her—nothing more, but he was still a man and had to guard against fleshly feelings.

He had no intention of being in love, not at this time of his life. He would just have to manage the best he could, trust in God, and keep his mind clear by prayer and scripture reading.

But he wished the best for Gus and deep in his heart believed that, because of Gus’s great faith, Christine would indeed come back to him.

No matter what others thought about it.

CHAPTER FIFTEEN

SLAMMING THE BACK DOOR, Ransom found his mother busy in the kitchen. It was early evening and he was hungry.

"Ransom! I've been wondering where you were. William and Jane came for dinner today. The Carroltons are here now for dessert. Are you hungry, dear?"

He nodded to her.

"We were just going to have some pie."

Ransom pulled back the chair with a scrape and turning it around, straddled his long-booted legs across it. His head rested on his folded arms across the back of the chair and he smiled as she chattered on. Mother loved having people around her.

As Elizabeth set silverware before him on the table, Rachel entered the room.

Rachel glanced his way without comment, then shifted her eyes toward Elizabeth.

Ransom took his arms from the back of the chair and looked at her. His heart began to beat a little faster and he said, "Hello, Rachel. How was your day? Were you able to make much sense of the Templeton Clan?"

Swinging her head toward him, this was the first word she had from him since she arrived. Rachel tried to answer, "I—I—"

Turning to Elizabeth, a little flustered, she asked, "Missus Templeton, could I help with the pie?"

"Oh, please, child! Call me Elizabeth. Yes, Rachel, get the small plates and put the pie on them."

As Rachel hurried to the cupboard, it was obvious to Ransom that she was more comfortable with his mother than anyone else. Not surprising, considering his mother's cheerfulness. She could charm the birds out of the trees.

Elizabeth was filled with excitement about the news of the day as she piled Ransom's plate with dinner leftovers.

She put a hand on her chest and closed her eyes. "William and Jane are going to have a baby! Imagine that!" Placing the plate before Ransom on the table, she said, "They just found out yesterday at Doctor Stone's office. Oh, I do so hope this baby will be a girl."

Ransom returned his chair to the proper position, sat down, and prepared to eat.

As she talked on, Ransom looked up and caught Rachel's eye. He smiled at her. Unnerved by his smile, she dropped a plate and it shattered into pieces.

Horrified, Rachel dropped her gaze to the floor. Nearly in tears at what she had done, she wanted to race up the kitchen stairway to her room, but, instead, began apologizing at once.

"Nonsense, Rachel," Elizabeth soothed. "There's nothing to apologize for. It can happen to anyone."

Elizabeth finished with the tray and gave Rachel instructions to serve in the parlor.

With as much grace as she could muster, Rachel took the tray and started for the other room.

Sitting in the parlor that evening, Ransom did his best to wrest his attention from Rachel and be engaging with Mr. and Mrs. Carrolton, but with little success.

A naturally witty person, Mrs. Carrolton was very entertaining and soft laughter escaped Rachel's lips at some comment she made.

Her laughter caught Ransom's attention. Rachel turned and saw his eyes resting on her with gentle amusement. She was immediately uncomfortable, thinking she had committed some impropriety again and that he was laughing at her. She looked away from him, embarrassed.

Since being subtlety informed by Elizabeth this morning of her atrocious table manners, she had felt insecure all day. It had been difficult enough when Jane asked prying questions. She was never sure whether she was doing or saying the right thing.

She didn't like this feeling. She wasn't even sure if she liked these people.

"What am I doing wrong? He keeps looking at me!" Rachel thought. "I know I'm not like these people. Maybe he thinks I'm some stupid country girl that doesn't have a lick of sense."

Feeling suddenly stifled by the room, Rachel stood up. She needed to escape to the outdoors.

Am I a prisoner in this house? Will they try to stop me?

She announced she was going for a walk.

"Oh, but it's almost dark!" Elizabeth exclaimed.

A determined look splashed across Rachel's face as she ignored Elizabeth's remark and started for the door.

At the look on Rachel's face, Elizabeth hurriedly said, "Ransom, go with Rachel, but don't be long," she fretted. "Rachel, put on one of my wraps hanging in the foyer. The air's turned cool and it wouldn't do for you to take a chill and get a fever from the night air."

Rachel nearly rolled her eyes. Take a chill indeed! Hunting, fishing, hands roughened by chopping wood, and breaking her young back working tirelessly in the fields was what she was accustomed to, particularly since Mother died. Elizabeth lived in a world much different than the one Rachel had known. But the role she was expected to play under the Templetons' care was that of a genteel young lady, and that, she was not.

Ransom took the paisley shawl off the hook and started to place it around her shoulders. Nearly snatching the garment from his hands, she was perturbed that he was going with her. She wanted to be alone. But she finally allowed him to drape the shawl over her.

At his touch, she found herself pulling away. Just why, she did not know.

CHAPTER SIXTEEN

STROLLING ALONG, Ransom dominated the conversation, relating the who's who of the town, and Rachel absently murmured hmm…at the appropriate times. She couldn't care less about the elite personage of Wellington's society and it was on the tip of her tongue to tell him so.

As they walked through town, Rachel closed her eyes and drew in a deep breath, savoring the familiar smells of the outdoors, a slight smile tugging at the corners of her mouth.

The dust of the street had settled down for the day, the residents were tucked away in their homes, and the only inhabitants to be seen were those few lounging about the inn. Except for the rustling of her silk dress, the firm steps of Ransom's boots and his rhythmic voice, the only other sound was the occasional clatter of gaiety from Wellington Saloon.

Ransom's soothing voice reminded her of Mother and stemming the tide of memories was impossible. Thoughts turned to Pa and where he might be at this moment. Was it only yesterday that he had left her? Some of the sense of bewilderment that pressed her since she arrived, pushed into the back of her mind, and in its place, an overwhelming wave of homesickness.

"I could leave in the middle of the night—run away," she thought. She stopped suddenly, her gaze fixed on some faraway place—her farm—and she gathered her skirts in her hands, ready to take flight.

Concerned, Ransom put a hand under Rachel's elbow and turned her toward him.

"Rachel?" he asked, puzzled.

Rachel gazed into his hazel eyes, as his soft voice drew her back to reality. What was that he was saying? He was there for her—he would help her through this trying time?

Her brow furrowed and she tried to pull away from him.

A whimper escaped her lips.

"Rachel," he urged, tugging her arm, "let's go home."

Home?

The parsonage was not home. Nor this town. Yes, she wanted to go home—home to the farm. Pulling against Ransom again, Rachel backed against the wall of Langdron's Store.

Through the terrifying miasma of her mind, only one thought became clear. Home! She could see it! If she could just get there! If she could just get there!

In a strangled voice Rachel cried, "Let me go! Let me go! I want to go home! Pa...don't leave me! Come back for me!"

Ransom pulled her hard against him, holding her tightly until her sobs subsided.

He loosened his hold only a little and his lips were buried in her disheveled hair, uttering soothing words...words she needed to hear...that someone loved her and cared for her.

What was that? He would take care of her? She could trust him? Trust...trust? Could she ever trust anyone again? The last few months of struggling against great odds had taken a toll on her. Suddenly, she was tired...tired of it all. She didn't want to fight or think anymore. She just wanted to lie down and sleep, and with that thought, she began to sag in his arms.

Slowly, Ransom relaxed his grasp and after what seemed an eternity, said, "I'll take you home now."

Home? Her home was at the farm. But she was not allowed to live there now.

There was no more fight left in her. She felt defeated by life—by its uncertainties—by its broken promises.

As Rachel leaned back against the wall, the wrap fell from her shoulders and she felt the roughness of crudely planed wood. Its prickly splinters jabbed through her dress, raked her skin, and pierced the dullness of her mind, forcing her to feel something...anything. She would go mad if she thought about her circumstances—it was a relief to focus on simple sensations.

She had tried to be strong for so many months, if not for herself, then Pa.

She had forced herself to put Mother out of her mind or she couldn't stand it. The vestiges of pain had torn at her heart for so long, but she'd found no time to grieve. Now the strength that had buoyed her up was gone.

CHAPTER SEVENTEEN

DETERMINED TO STAY WITH RACHEL through the night, Ransom avoided his parents' questions. "She's just trying to adjust," was all he would tell them, dismissing their inquiries with a wave of his hand and the promise of later discussion. He would talk to Father tomorrow, but tonight, he would not leave Rachel.

Jacob's eyebrows rose at Ransom's answer. After all, Rachel was his ward, not Ransom's. Jacob opened his mouth to speak but his arguments were stilled by the pleading look in Ransom's eyes. Setting his jaw, Jacob silently consented with a slow nod and steered Elizabeth away from Rachel's room.

"But why can't I know what's going on?" Elizabeth asked while attempting to stall in front of Rachel's door.

"Just leave Ransom alone. When he's ready to talk—he will."

"But I don't think it's proper," she argued, "for he and Rachel to be alone in her bedchamber."

"Elizabeth, you know as well as I, that bundling goes on all the time. No one will say a word."

Though Jacob didn't actually approve of the courting practice of two young people spending a night alone together in a bedroom, either sewed in individual sacks or with merely a board placed in middle of the bed between them, still, it was a custom that was commonly practiced.

Even so, Jacob trusted his son to be on his best behavior.

Rachel slept fitfully that night. Ransom pulled the armchair beside her bed, watching her. He could not allow her to wake and do something foolish like take off in the dark for her farm for he knew that was exactly what she had in mind.

He prayed silently beside her for a long time that night. "Lord, I know if we show her your love, she will come to know and trust you for who you are. She's scared and doesn't trust anyone right now. Give me the strength and wisdom to meet this situation."

The plight she was thrust into was not a trial he had ever borne. He had always considered himself blessed, surrounded by strong and loving parents who made him feel secure. However, he could understand that despite his parents' goodness, they were still strangers to Rachel.

Wrenched from her home at a moment's notice, leaving all she knew, how frightened, lonely, and hurt she must be!

Ransom's head came up with a jerk. How long he had slept he did not know. He had not meant to fall asleep and was awakened with a start by Rachel's cries, for she awoke, frightened, and sobbing brokenly.

Ransom moved to the side of the bed and put his arm under her head, gathered her to him—cradling her while murmuring soothing sounds until her sobbing ceased and lapsed into the steady, rhythmic breathing of sleep. Then he gently disengaged himself and settled back into the armchair, relieved she was finally resting.

As Ransom watched Rachel sleeping, he was torn. He longed to reach out and touch her, but he dared not. He felt so mixed up. He wanted to go and yet he wanted to stay.

"Lord, what to do?" he prayed desperately. "I've got feelings for this girl and I don't even know her. I can't ignore her either, for Father has entrusted me with the responsibility of her studies."

Ransom needed some time to collect his thoughts before ever being alone with her again. Funny, how things seemed so simple before. He could not recall spending so much time in earnest prayer. But he now found himself in almost constant prayer, asking for renewed strength and continual guidance. Assured of himself in the past, he was now in uncharted territory.

Will's lumber mill was located on the outskirts of town. Ransom had worked full time for Will and part time in the afternoons when school was in session. The mill had become the place where men exchanged small talk or just got away from their wives and the younger men came because Ransom was there.

As the mill grew busier with the spring season in full swing, Will often lingered after it closed to fill orders. Jane knew her husband was success-driven and tolerated his ambition for a while after they were married. However, the extra-long hours began to mar the relationship between the two of them, so occasionally, he asked Ransom to stay in his place.

Suddenly, the solution occurred to him and he sat straight up in the chair. "That's it! She can come to the mill a couple of hours a day for study. It's a public place and I won't have to spend so much time in private with her. Problem solved!"

"Uh—oh," he thought as a frown wrinkled his forehead and he slumped back in the chair. "I've got to deal with Father and Mother. I can probably get Father to go along with this, but Mother's a different matter. She will insist that it is inappropriate. Oh, well, I'll just have to do my best to convince her."

As the sun began to show itself over the hills that lay beyond the perimeters of Wellington, a weary Ransom stretched his arms over his head, stifling a yawn. In spite of efforts to stay awake, he had dozed off again. He looked down at Rachel and saw she was awake and quietly watching him.

"Good morning, sleepyhead," he said with a grin.

Rachel said nothing. Watching him with an inscrutable look, she barely blinked as he wearily massaged the back of his neck. She wondered if he had stayed with her all night. As the room began to glow with the soft morning light creeping through the slats of the shuttered window, she had a faint recollection of being in Ransom's arms.

Color crept into her cheeks as she remembered his soft voice against her ear, and words spoken in the night, words that a lover might speak, loving expressions of a longing heart finding its release in the intimacy of darkness. Words—so private and unspeakable. She was his dark-eyed beauty, he had claimed. She had never heard such words before.

The look in her eyes pressed him on.

"What is it?" he questioned, almost in a whisper.

Ransom knew even as he asked. Her eyes told him so. Hoping that she hadn't remembered last night was futile. She remembered but said nothing.

For an instant, the silence was so acute it seemed neither of them breathed.

She looked away and then broke the awkward silence. Slipping her arm from under the coverlet, "Were—were you here *all* night?" she asked.

Rubbing a face that needed a shave, "Yes, I was," he answered.

For some reason she knew he would say yes. Why he was concerned about her welfare was puzzling.

Drawing in a deep breath, "I'm sorry," she apologized. "I didn't mean to put you to so much trouble."

"No trouble."

The anxiety of the last few moments dissipated as the change came over her. Strength and determination lit her face as she attempted to sit up. Her head was now clear and her intention strong. Moaning about her situation would do no good and the time for crying was past.

"I promise I won't try to run away," Rachel assured him in a dismissive tone and busied herself adjusting the coverlet, rallying her forces into a semblance of dignity.

"Good!" he replied nonchalantly, as rising to his full height, he pushed the chair back into the corner. "I'm going to try to get a couple of hours of sleep. I'm sure Delcey is here by now. She'll cook you some breakfast. I'll see you later today."

He began striding toward the door. He'd been good to her and she needed to thank him. Everything within her wanted to call him back.

She nearly didn't. Her heart finally pushed through the numbness of her lips.

"Ransom?"

With his hand on the knob, he turned.
“Thanks,” she whispered softly.

CHAPTER EIGHTEEN

IT WAS MONDAY AND, AS PROMISED, ELIZABETH was going to take Rachel to Langdron's Store for complete outfitting of her wardrobe. Jane and Cissa had agreed to accompany them. If there was anything Elizabeth enjoyed more than receiving gifts, it was shopping. She knew the girls would not arrive until about ten o'clock and spent the morning preparing the list of all they would buy today.

"Let's see," she remarked going over her list with Rachel. "Material, thread, hooks and eyes, shoes, and of course we want to see the very latest patterns they have!"

Ransom came down the stairs just as Jane and Cissa entered the door.

"Hey, Ransom!" Jane said as she crossed the foyer to give him a hug. "You're getting a late start today!" Glancing at the clock on the mantle, she said, "It's ten o'clock. You're usually at the mill before now. Did you have a late night?" Jane teased.

"You're mighty nosy today!" he quipped back. "Talk about late nights…I hear you and Will are expecting." Landing a peck on her cheek, he grinned, "Congratulations, Jane."

Rachel looked up from the shopping list in shock! Hearing such talk, her mouth dropped open and a blush crept over her face. In all her years, such a thing was never heard between Mother and Pa! Such talk, so private and unspeakable!

"What kind of family did Pa leave me with?" Rachel wondered, appalled, and cast her eyes down.

"Thanks, Ransom. Or should I say, Uncle Ransom?" Jane asked, her cheeks flashing their dimpling.

"You little minx. You may. I'll be glad to be an uncle. How's Will with all this?"

"Oh, he's absolutely thrilled. Of course, his mind is made up it will be a son. Already got the name picked out—Jacob, after your father."

"I'm sure Father will be pleased to hear that. But..." His eyes twinkling, he said thoughtfully, "perhaps you'd better pick out a name if it's a girl."

Drawing his ear to her mouth, "We have," she whispered. "It's Elizabeth. But don't tell your mother. If it's a girl, we want her to be surprised."

He laughed. "Oh, she'll be surprised all right."

Was it his imagination or was Rachel blushing?

Yes, she was. Rachel was definitely blushing.

"Ransom," Cissa said, "has James asked you to be part of the wedding party yet?"

"Umm...what's that?" he asked, pulling his mind, but not his eyes, back from their distraction. "Oh, yes, Cissa, but we never got into details."

"Well, it's only a couple of months away. Wait until you see my dress!" she said enthusiastically.

Ransom looked away from Rachel to Cissa standing at his elbow. "I'm sure on you it's beautiful, Cissa," he said, a gentle smile on his face.

Elizabeth walked into the hall. Putting on her hat, she peered in the mirror. "Let's go, girls," she announced, pulling on her gloves. "We have a lot of shopping to do."

Jacob was in the library and Ransom opened the door after a short knock.

"May I come in, Father?" he asked.

Jacob laid down his quill and moved the inkpot farther from his sheet of foolscap. "Sure, son." Ransom stepped in and took a chair across from the desk.

"What's on your mind, Ransom?" Jacob asked.

"If you don't care, Father," he asked, "may if I wait a day or two before I begin tutoring Rachel?"

"Is there anything wrong?" asked Jacob, a questioning look in his eyes.

Rising from the chair and moving toward the window, Ransom brushed back the drapes and finally answered, "No. I just need to think some things through."

"Things?" Jacob questioned. "What sort of things, Ransom?"

Ransom looked down, studying his hands. "Um...oh, just some things. I have a favor to ask of you. So often I work late at the mill, as you know. Would it be all right if Rachel came there a couple of hours a day for study?"

"Do you think that's the proper place for Rachel to be?"

Turning back toward the desk, Ransom sighed heavily. "Frankly, I don't know, Father. I'll keep her in the office away from the other men, for sure. Without giving you much explanation, I'm asking, please, for my sake, go along with this."

"I don't know what's going through your mind, Ransom," Jacob remarked, pulling on his ear, "but apparently you're having some sort of struggle."

Drumming his fingers on the desk, he asked, "Does it have anything to do with Rachel?"

Ransom didn't answer.

"Well, evidently it does." Jacob thought for a few moments. "I realize Rachel is different in every way, unique, as a matter of fact. But I suppose that is part of her charm. And I also realize she's struggling to find her place. She's had a tough time and needs us all."

Jacob crossed his arms. "Against my better judgment, I'll give my consent, but you realize you'll have to convince your mother and, more importantly, Will. After all, it is *his* business."

Ransom hadn't taken into consideration what Will would say about it. Of course, Father was right. It was his business and Will could be hot-headed and a formidable adversary when he chose to be. Ransom felt like a rabbit in a trap and he desperately needed to escape the emotional entanglement he was feeling. Somehow, he had to convince his family that tutoring Rachel at the mill was the right decision. Tonight, after dinner, he will lay out his best argument.

CHAPTER NINETEEN

WILL AND RANSOM BOTH ENJOYED THE HARD WORK of the mill, but their real talent lay in crafting fine furnishings. Furniture was not readily transported into the county and they found great demand for their works of art. Will knew the ladies were uncomfortable frequenting the mill for their purchases and hearing their complaints, on more than one occasion, he toyed with the idea of building a store in town specifically to sell their much in demand furniture. He needed Ransom's talents but would soon be losing him to the university, so he was considering asking James to help. James was spending a lot of time with Cissa preparing for their wedding. He was also getting his own home ready for his bride, in addition to spending time in ministry with their father. Yes, it was probably best to approach him after the wedding when he was more settled, he surmised.

Arriving home that evening, Ransom found Will and James there with Cissa and Jane. Paper wrappings had been hastily thrown in a heap after yielding up their contents. Barely had he stepped inside the door when Elizabeth went to him.

"There you are, Ransom. We're almost ready to sit down to dinner."

He hung his coat and she pulled him into the parlor. "Oh! What a day we have had! Just wait 'til you see the beautiful things we bought for Rachel today! Look! These two fashionable dresses. They fit her perfectly! Satin shoes, leather shoes, fine stockings, white kid gloves and a beautiful Persian quilted coat! A corset and cap and oh, so many garments, plus material and patterns and egrettes and ribbon—"

"Mother, do you think she'll wear all of these things?" Ransom frowned and threw a sidelong glance at Jacob. "She's not used to them, you know."

"What girl wouldn't want to wear these beautiful things?" she asked, surprised.

"Just don't be disappointed," he warned.

She was determined that Rachel *would* wear these things in spite of Ransom's warning.

"Oh, goodness!" Elizabeth suddenly said. "Dinner is getting cold! We'd better sit down to eat."

"Let me wash up first, Mother," Ransom replied.

As he bounded up the stairs, he met Rachel coming down.

"Hello, Rachel."

She nodded. As she moved to pass him, he laid his hand on her arm, causing her to pause.

"I want to ask you something while I have you alone."

A questioning look crossed her face.

"I was wondering—would you consider coming to the mill around noon each day for your studies? Often I'm a little late coming home at night and I thought it might be better if we spent a couple of hours each day in the office there."

At the mill? What's a mill? Rachel wanted to ask him. She felt awkward and tongue-tied. "I guess so," she replied, instead.

Casting a wide smile, he said, "Good. I've got to wash up." And with that he raced up the stairs.

At dinner Ransom was quiet as the chatter of his family turned its direction toward Rachel.

"You know, Rachel," Cissa said, "Jane and I have been talking and since she found that she's expecting, we wondered if you would take her place in the wedding party."

Rachel drew her breath in sharply and her fork clattered against the plate. "Me?"

They nodded their heads in agreement.

Picking up the fork as resistance curled her lip, "I—I don't know," she stammered. "I've never seen a wedding before."

With eyebrows raised, the girls chimed in unison, "Never?"

"Well, no matter. We'll have practice before the wedding and

I'm sure you'll have no problem," Jane assured her. "We're trying to decide the color of dress for you. Yellow is the popular color right now. Fortunately, with your complexion you can wear any color. You're so pretty, and of course, Ransom will be your escort."

Things were moving too fast for her liking. Annoyed, if someone considered her to be backwoods, she now applied the term to herself. New places, new things, new responsibilities—it was all a little frightening.

Glancing at Ransom from the corner of her eye, she found he was watching her and gave her an almost imperceptible nod.

"Of course," she responded faintly.

Jacob, Elizabeth, James, Will, and Ransom gathered in the library later at Ransom's request. Clearing his throat, he said, "I wanted to ask permission of you, Mother, that Rachel might be spared a couple of hours a day for her studies, preferably at noon at the mill. I've already talked to Father about it and he agrees if you and Will are willing."

"The mill?" Elizabeth questioned with a shocked look. "But that's where the men gather!"

Ransom looked down and answered as nonchalantly as possible, "Yes, I know, but it's more convenient for me as I work late some days and I'll make sure the office where we'll study is off limits to them."

Will was appalled at such an idea and, immediately up in arms, yelled, "Are you out of your mind, Ransom? Bring a girl down there? You know what it's like with men coming and going all day! We'll be the talk of the town."

Frustrated, Ransom retorted, "When did you ever care about what people think of us, Will?"

Soft-spoken James spoke up, "Will's right, Ransom. We've always enjoyed a good reputation in this town, and more importantly, what about Rachel's reputation? Have you considered her? Do you realize how people will gossip about her? Call her morally loose?"

Elizabeth, for once, was at a loss for words. What would people say? Rachel had been placed under their protective care and to allow her to be in a place where men gathered was unthinkable. They had their position to consider. Jacob was pastor of the church and the gossip would bring both he and the rest of the family under scrutiny.

"She'll be in my care," Ransom argued. "I'll keep her from the men. It'll work out. You'll see. I'll make sure of that. It's just that she's not used to being shut up in this house all the time. Rachel needs to be in a different environment."

"Different environment?" Will sputtered. "She'll still be shut up inside down there. You're not making any sense, Ransom."

Elizabeth sought Jacob's eyes. At her unspoken question, he gave a resigned look.

For several minutes the brothers argued and pleaded and protested, but Ransom remained steadfast in his request.

An angry Will stormed out flinging words over his shoulder, "Fine! I don't know what your *real* problem is, Ransom. You can bring Rachel down there if that's what you are intent on doing, but any consequences that come from this will be laid at *your* door!"

CHAPTER TWENTY

UPON ENTERING THE MILL, AT NOON, THE NEXT DAY, Rachel was pleasantly surprised by the smell of lumber. This made her feel immediately at home and a smile widened her face. Over her arm was a basket sent by Elizabeth packed with their lunch.

Will was standing by several men who were sitting on handcrafted stools just outside the office door. Noticing Rachel, he came walking toward her, a frown furrowing his forehead.

"Hello, Rachel." Although his words were cordial, his tone was not. "Ready for your studies today?"

Rachel nodded. She was shy around Will. His candor was intimidating. Holding the basket out to him, she said, "Umm…Elizabeth sent lunch."

"Thanks, Rachel." Taking the basket from her arm, he declared, "I'm starved. Ransom's in the back room." Pointing that way, he asked, "Would you tell him lunch is here?"

Skirting around the wood chips on the floor, she made her way toward the back room and taking a wary step across the threshold, she was met by all kind of furniture: tables, chairs, hutches, bookcases, settees, and chairs ready to be upholstered. Nothing like the few crude pieces in the cabin on her farm, but truly fine craftsmanship.

A soft "Oh!" escaped her lips.

Ransom stepped from behind a large piece he was working on.

"Ransom, how beautiful!"

"Like it?" he asked.

"Like it! When—how long—where did you learn to do this?"

A warm feeling came over him and he colored slightly at the obvious sincerity of her words. "Oh, Will and I have been doing this for a few years," he said offhandedly. "Sometimes James helps. We've sold quite a few pieces, actually."

As Rachel caressed the top of a chair, she murmured, "You know,

Pa taught me how to whittle. I would love to learn to do this." Suddenly, jerking her head up and looking at him, she asked excitedly, "Oh, Ransom, would you teach me? I'm a quick learner and I just *know* I can do this!"

Ransom smiled as he got a true glimpse of the girl who would barely say two words to him before. For one rash moment he was tempted to give in to her request. Then shaking his head in an attempt to thwart her sudden ambition, he said, "Now, *wait,* Rachel. This is man's work. Besides, you'll get your new clothes torn and dirty."

Rachel would not be refused. She bit her lip as she thought. Looking at his pants, she said, "Loan me a pair of your breeches and a shirt. I can wear those."

His eyes opened wide. "Pants?"

Rachel put her hands on her hips and looked up at him. "Sure. I wore them a lot on the farm." She tossed her head. "Pa not only let me, but he liked it when I wore pants."

Ransom put his hands on his hips, too, and shook his head. "Well, you're in town now, Rachel. People don't approve of women wearing trousers."

"Pooh!" Rachel said with an airy wave of her hand. "What do I care what people say! I'll do what I want. Let them talk!"

He hooked his thumbs in his waist. "My breeches won't fit you, anyway. They're too big."

She frowned. Then: "I'll ask Elizabeth to cut them down or to make me a pair."

Right, Ransom thought. *There's a better chance of pigs flying than that happening.*

Suddenly, Rachel's face lit up. "Better still! I'll go to the farm and get my own! Yes, that's what I'll do!" Crossing to where he was standing, she took his arm and looked up at him. "Take me, will you, Ransom?" she begged. "We could go this evening. It won't take long and I'm not afraid of the dark."

He threw up his hands trying to ward off the persuasive note in her voice. She had been up and down emotionally since she arrived. He'd seen her determined spirit, but the naked emotional appeal on her face right now was too much. Her large eyes were drawing him in and everything within him was on the edge of granting her anything.

Ransom leaned back away from her and shook his head as he tried to clear it. Throwing up his hands again, he said, "Now, Rachel. This isn't proper for a girl," he argued. "Stick to sewing and things like that. Besides, you'll ruin your hands."

"Ruin my hands?" she said incredulously.

"Look at my hands!" She held them in the air, palms forward for him to see. "They're blistered and callused already!"

Ransom gently took her hands, lowered them, turned them over and studied the hardened wounds that covered them. A large, glaring scar, the result of a burn, was seared across one palm. He closed his hands over her small ones.

Without raising his head, in a quiet voice, he asked, "What happened, Rachel?"

Wincing, she tried to pull her hands away, but he refused to relinquish them. Slowly raising his head, "Look at me!" he said.

His hazel eyes had darkened to slate gray. "I asked, what happened, Rachel! Tell me!"

Rachel didn't want to talk about the past. That was between her and Pa. She did not want him to know the intimate details of her life and especially that Pa had been sick. The harsh memories were quickly becoming buried deep in her heart and she didn't want to stir them up again.

She squirmed and tried again to free herself from his firm grasp, regretting she had impetuously displayed her hands for him to see.

His jaw tightened and in a quiet voice, he said, "I won't let you go until you tell me what has happened."

She did not doubt it.

Looking away from him, she said, "I don't want to talk about it, Ransom."

"I realize that," he replied. "But I need to know."

Need to know? Why should he be interested in her past and what good would it do, anyway? She felt disloyal speaking about Pa and yet she could not deny that anger still smoldered deep in the recesses of her heart. How could she tell him about the last few months? She did not want to cry—she had cried in front of him enough already. She did not want to appear weak and needy, either, for she had always been strong and willful.

But what was it about this man that could make her bend to his will? Her resolve was weakening, and she felt almost angry that he was forcing the memories of the recent past to the forefront again.

Ransom watched the expressions of conflict cross her face.

"All right!" she finally said and jerked her hands away. "I'll tell you!"

Turning from him, Rachel disclosed everything that had happened, beginning with the death of her mother until the day she came to live with them.

Somewhere deep inside Ransom grew a feeling of hurt for the bruised and fractured childhood of this beautiful girl. But more than that…a deep respect for the strength of character she had. She took the challenges of life head on, not murmuring or whimpering as others might and forced those challenges to bow to her own will. And even with a broken heart, she had not given up and became the nurturer for her own father, instead.

How strange this girl—great strength and yet great vulnerability all in one. Never had he met anyone who possessed so much of both.

Feeling as though a weight had lifted from her, she talked of her free-spirited father who encouraged her to be the same, how he had taught her to hunt and fish and live as one with the land.

Ransom now understood her earthiness. It was her connection with nature that made her unique. She did not wear a facade like so many girls he knew. She was who she was, accepted or not.

Swinging around to face him, she caught him watching her with a look she could not quite fathom.

Vehemently, she said, "Don't pity me! I can't stand that!"

"I don't pity you," he said with a half-smile on his face. "I respect you."

Wide-eyed, she stammered, "You—you respect me?"

"Yes." Putting his hands on his hips, he said, "and I'll make you an apprentice. Now what do you think about that?"

She thought a moment. "What's an apprentice?" she asked, wrinkling her brow.

"An apprentice, dear girl, is one who learns a trade under another who is skilled."

"Oh." Pausing, trying to make sense of what he had just said. "You will?" her face lighting with a smile. "And you really think I can learn?" Rachel asked, her face shining with eagerness.

"Yes." He smiled. "Now, see how you get your way when you open up to me?"

Will stuck his head in the door. "Hey! I thought you were coming to lunch."

Losing her shyness, Rachel rushed over excitedly and grabbed his arm. "Oh, Will!" she exclaimed breathlessly. "Ransom is going to make me an apprentice. He's going to teach me to make furniture."

"He is?" His eyes widened, his eyebrows rose, and skepticism was written on his face.

"Yes, and he's going to take me to the farm to pick up some clothes."

An unnerving thought suddenly struck Ransom. "I've made this promise to Rachel and haven't even consulted with Mother or Father!" he groaned.

Ransom felt he was being drawn deeper into something he could not stop. Not only did he seem to be becoming a commanding force in Rachel's life, but she seemed to be able to wield her own will on his. Instead of becoming insulted by this, he felt strangely exhilarated by it.

Replaying their conversation in his mind, he chuckled to himself as he started for the office. "One thing for sure, Rachel has a way of getting what she wants!"

Rachel was still excited and the men sitting nearby could not help but overhear—and they didn't like what they heard. This was a man's world, and the mill was no place for women. They nearly spoke their piece. But at the warning frown on Will's face, they kept their thoughts to themselves, although the looks that passed between them predicted this would bring nothing but trouble.

CHAPTER TWENTY-ONE

"WHAT? NO! THAT IS COMPLETELY OUT OF THE QUESTION!" Elizabeth came out of her chair in a flash and waving her arms, swooped on Ransom like a bird protecting its young.

"What will people say about Rachel *and* us? She has to learn to be a lady."

With another wave, Elizabeth furiously uttered, "Not some wild child out of control. I'm having a hard time enough getting her to wear some of the items of clothing I bought her. Rachel balks about wearing a corset and she *absolutely* refuses to wear a cap or even a bonnet. I may be able to talk her into wearing her white kid gloves…at least on Sunday. I'm trying to reform her so that she'll fit in with society."

Shaking her head and folding her arms, she stated emphatically, "I am willing to make some concessions, but this is going too far. No. Absolutely not! I won't hear of it, Ransom!

"I should never have agreed to let her go to the mill!" she moaned, throwing her hands in the air.

"I know how you feel, Mother, but Rachel is different," Ransom pleaded. "And she needs this. She's an outdoors girl and working with wood will help her feel connected with nature and the sense of who she is."

He set his jaw. "And in spite of what you think, Mother, Rachel *is* a lady."

Jacob had little to say. It had come as a shock to him as well. When Ransom brought up the subject of Rachel wearing trousers, Elizabeth's face went white and Jacob thought she would pass out on the spot. One thing was certain, he was convinced the Council would not understand and the congregation of his church would give them a hard time over it.

"She's just unpretentious, Mother, and doesn't care what people say about her," Ransom campaigned on. "Besides, she'll only wear them at the mill."

Elizabeth pointed her finger at him. "Well, I *do* care! I am telling you, Ransom, it's not fitting. It's just *not* fitting."

Letting out an exasperated breath, Ransom sank down in the chair and put his head in his hands.

Jacob sat quietly in the large brown, damask, wing-backed chair while Ransom pleaded his case to Elizabeth. He had never denied Ransom much. Never saw the need to, for Ransom had always been so level-headed.

He, himself, was torn as to the best course of action. He had never seen Ransom so headstrong about anything before now and he questioned his son's judgment.

Quietly, Jacob remarked, "Ransom, I've always let you make your own decisions. But, son, you should have asked us first before making this promise to Rachel. After all, you must remember, we are her guardians."

Raising his head with a nod of agreement, Ransom said remorsefully, "I know, Father. I promised before thinking about you and Mother and you are right. I should have sought your permission first."

"Well, seeing that you admit your mistake...."

Jacob paused thoughtfully for a few moments, then turned to his wife. "Elizabeth, I'm going to side with Ransom on this. I know you want to turn Rachel into a parody of the other girls—don't glare at me, Elizabeth—you know it's true—but she *is* different. I prefer to think of her as God's special child. If you try to change her too quickly, she will rebel. Try to be more subtle, dear. Teach her things such as sewing and the etiquette of young ladies, but let her have her head, too. Who knows? Maybe God has a special calling on someone like Rachel."

"Mother, Father," Ransom interrupted, "Rachel told me today about what she's gone through the last few months. Have you noticed her hands?"

As Ransom related Rachel's confessions, tears welled in Elizabeth's eyes and she finally blurted out, "I need to ask God for forgiveness. I've misjudged this girl. You are right, Jacob. We will stand behind her whether she's conventional or not and let her be herself, and God give us the grace to bear what we have to bear."

Rachel waited eagerly for Ransom to take her to her farm.

He walked into the room and she jumped up from the settee and said she was ready to go.

"Not tonight, Rachel. Mother doesn't want us travelling after dark and I need to talk to Will tonight. You can walk over with me if you want. We'll leave tomorrow morning after breakfast."

She was disappointed, but not for long. Whirling in a circle, she stopped in front of him and placed her hands on his arms. "Oh, thank you, Ransom. You've made me *so* happy!" He looked down at her from his height of six feet and her shining eyes melted him as he realized it didn't take much to please her.

"We'll see Will after dinner, and I'll tell you a little about furniture making. By the way, did you know Will is talking about building a furniture store in town?"

"Really!" She let go of his arms and thought about that. Chewing on her lip, she suddenly blurted out, "Maybe he'll let me work in his store."

Instantly, he groaned and wished he had kept his mouth shut. He threw back his head and gave a disapproving laugh. "Slow down, Rachel. Don't forget, your number one priority right now is education."

She laughed impertinently. Gathering her skirts, she waltzed dreamily in front of him. "So much to do. Studies, furniture making, clothes, and tomorrow we're going home."

She stood still and looking up, she spoke with uncertainty in her voice, "Ransom?"

"Don't worry, Rachel," he reassured. "I'll be there."

CHAPTER TWENTY-TWO

WILL WAS UPSET BY RANSOM'S DECISION to allow Rachel to work at the mill and he related this to Jane as they finished dinner.

Jane was horrified. "What are you going to do, Will? It would be disgraceful for her to work there. This town will give her a hard time, especially our congregation. And what about my father? He's on the Council, too. Think what position that will put him in."

He shrugged his shoulders. "What can I do? It's too late now."

Her voice raised a notch. "*You're* the owner. What you say goes."

He rose from the table and she followed him into the parlor where he sat down in his favorite chair.

"It's not quite that simple," he said. "If it was anyone other than family, it would be a different matter."

Jane snorted.

He raised a hand. "Don't say anything to Rachel if that's what's going through your mind. The best way to handle this is to let it play itself out."

She looked at him sternly. "Play itself out? You don't take that kind of approach with *me*! You're the head of the house and you sure don't let *me* forget it!"

"That's different. You're my wife."

Her temper began to rise. "I may be your wife, but one day you'll find out, William Templeton, that I'm not some collateral like your business. I know you are success-driven, but I've got feelings, too, and you can't treat me like you do your business."

He sighed and rubbed his eyes. "Let's don't get into this now, Jane. I've had a rough day and I'm dog-tired."

There was a knock at the door and when she answered it, Jane was surprised to see Ransom and Rachel standing there.

Rachel was lending a hand with the dishes when Jane musingly brought up Rachel's latest venture. Will had warned her to stay out of it, but Jane felt duty-bound to advise Rachel woman to woman.

"Rachel, Will told me tonight that you're going to work in the mill."

Rachel set down the plate she was drying and turned to Jane, her eyes sparkling. "Oh, yes, Jane! Isn't it exciting? Have you seen the beautiful furniture they've made?" Closing her eyes, she smiled. "I just love the smell of that place."

Jane handed Rachel another plate, eyeing her with disapproval. "That's fine, Rachel, but have you considered how the town will talk about you working there?"

"A little." She frowned as she took the plate and gave a swipe.

Shrugging her shoulders, Rachel declared, "But I don't really care."

Setting the plate down, she asked, "Why should they be concerned about what I do, anyway?"

"The problem is—they'll think you're appearing unladylike. When men get ready to marry, they look for ladies to become betrothed to and they consider helplessness part of being a lady."

"Why?" Rachel asked quizzically, as she leaned against the sink.

"It makes them feel strong, like they're the protector." Jane sighed. "They have such big egos."

"What do you mean?" Rachel drew her brows together, intrigued by this bit of news.

Jane handed Rachel a handful of rinsed silverware. "They think it's important to be the provider and want to feel they excel in their manhood. And they want someone to compliment them. They like women to make them feel they're better than other men."

Rachel snorted. "That's silly! Don't women have egos?"

"Yes, I suppose so." Jane paused to think about that. "But we're taught to attain our identity through a man. You know…get married and have children."

Flipping the towel on the sink, Rachel's voice rose. "So, you're saying I can't be what I am…I have to pretend to be what a man thinks I am. Right?"

"Yes, that's right! You've got it!" Jane was smugly satisfied that Rachel finally understood.

"Huh! Well, I'll tell you right now, they can keep it! If that's what it takes to get married, I just won't bother," Rachel stated with finality and picked the towel back up.

Disappointed, Jane turned back to the pot she was scrubbing. "I just wanted you to be warned, the women can get spiteful and," lowering her voice, she whispered, "men can be cruel, especially when they're after—well, you know."

"What are you talking about, Jane?" Rachel asked.

Jane's eyebrows rose. "You don't know?"

Rachel turned to look at Jane. "Should I?"

"Sweetie, just how old *are* you?"

Rachel was slow to answer as she wondered what age had to do with anything. "Fifteen, almost sixteen."

"Honey, you'd better have a talk with Elizabeth. She'll tell you about life."

"Well, if that's life, I'm not sure if I'm interested enough to know," she declared with a snort.

Rising just after sunrise, Ransom made his way to the kitchen. He gave a start when Rachel appeared in the doorway, dressed, and anxious to leave.

"Good morning," he said, stifling a yawn.

"Good morning, Ransom. I'm ready to go whenever you are." Her hands were clasped behind her back and a big smile spread across her face as she rocked back and forth on her heels.

"Yes, I can see." Already regretting that he had risen so early, he asked, "Well, how about we rustle a little breakfast before we start out? We'd better think about packing lunch, too."

Rachel wrinkled up her face. "Hmm...you're right. I never gave that a thought. You start breakfast and I'll pack lunch. Let's see," she put her finger to her cheek, "I wonder what's in the springhouse."

Ransom put a few sticks of wood in the stove that his parents had recently purchased and, before long, had a fire going.

As Rachel scurried around the kitchen, chattering happily, Delcey walked through the back door. "What's going on? Why are you two up so early?"

"We're going on a little trip, Delcey," Ransom informed her. "I'm trying to fix a little breakfast and Rachel is packing lunch for us."

"Well, never you mind. I'll fix the breakfast while you finish getting dressed." And with that she pulled an apron out of the drawer.

"Thanks, Delcey. Be back in a few moments, Rachel."

"Where are you going today, child?" Delcey asked as she took down a bowl from the cupboard.

Excitedly, Rachel answered, "We're going to my farm to pick up some work clothes."

Delcey put the ingredients to make flapjacks in the bowl and walked to the sink. "Work clothes?" she asked absently.

"Yes. Ransom is going to teach me to make furniture at the mill and I need some pants to work in."

Her eyes wide, Delcey turned and asked, "Pants? And you're learning furniture making?" She shook her head. "Mmm…mmm…mmm! What'd the Reverend and Missus Templeton have to say about that?"

"Oh, they've agreed." She sat down and put her elbows on the table and her chin in her hands. "They think it will be good for me."

Delcey spent a few minutes, while she stirred, going over the pros and cons of such a decision with Rachel.

Pouring the batter into the skillet, she warned, "It's none of my business…but you know, honey, the people in this town will talk."

Rachel did not like the way the conversation had drifted and began to pout as she drew imaginary circles on the table. "What difference does it make?" she asked, pulling her face into a frown.

"It's what I want to do and why should people care, anyway?"

"That's just the way folks are, always sticking their nose in somebody else's business." With a shake of her head, she said, "Anyhow, it's your decision. Just don't get hurt by it."

Ransom walked through the kitchen toward his boots when her last sentence struck a chord in him. Don't get hurt! Pulling on his boots, he thought, "I'll have to have a heart-to-heart talk with Rachel today. If she is bound and determined to go through with this, then I want her prepared."

CHAPTER TWENTY-THREE

RANSOM DECIDED THEY WOULD TAKE THE BUGGY. He needed the closeness to talk to her.

Passing by the turnoff to the river, he said, "I'd like to show you the river some time, Rachel. It's where our church baptisms take place, and I've often gone there to fish or just to pray. It's right through that thicket," he said, pointing.

"Oh, I'd like that, Ransom! I used to go fishing with Pa a lot."

"Does it bother you to bait your hook?"

"Oh, no! I don't need help with that. Pa taught me so much. When Pa was sick, I would shoot deer for our food. Although," she continued with a roll of her eyes, "I must say I didn't care much for dressing it."

They rode along in silence for a while, neither uncomfortable by the lapse of conversation. She loved being outdoors. It lifted her spirits. The trees were completely leaved out now. She had not taken much notice of them on her ride to town with Pa, so upset she had been. The different shades of green complimented and blended with one another and the birds, preparing nests to lay their eggs in, were singing their own unique songs. Spring was in full bloom and life was worth living.

Ransom cut into her thoughts with a solemn note in his voice.

"Rachel?"

"Hmm?" she answered absently.

"I know you're determined to go through with this, but I want you to realize what you're getting into."

Rachel turned and looked at him. "What do you mean?"

"Well, though people can have good intentions—even Christians—understand that sometimes they can act mean and cruel and in their own way think they are standing for what is right."

"What are you talking about, Ransom?"

"The townspeople are not going to understand you working at the mill and they will talk about you."

"I know." A rabbit scurried across the road and momentarily caught her attention. "More than one person has told me that."

"But you don't understand, Rachel. They will separate themselves from you and look down on you."

She waved her hand in an air of dismissal. "I know."

"You still don't understand. You've lived a sheltered life and haven't been exposed to the cruelty of others."

"My pa left me...didn't he?" she asked softly.

Thoughtfully, he answered, "Yes...and I realize you're hurting and having a hard time dealing with that. But that is not what I'm talking about. People will hurt you for reasons known only to them. It is not easy for them to accept people who live or think differently than they do. I'm just telling you that people are going to talk about you behind your back and I don't want you to get hurt."

She laid her hand on his arm. "But, Ransom, you've never been hurt by these people, have you?"

"No, not so much. But I grew up among them and I know their weaknesses as well as their strengths and I accept them as they are and leave it up to God to make any changes that need to be made. But that way of thinking doesn't come overnight and so I choose the right time to take a stand and voice my opinion. I love them in spite of their weaknesses just as Christ loves me in spite of mine. Scripture says, *All have sinned and come short of the glory of God. There is none righteous, no not one.* We are made righteous by God's righteousness. Does that make any sense to you, Rachel?"

She turned back to look at the road. "Yes...a little. Mother used to read scripture and tell me how loving God is. She told me that God would not put upon me more than I can bear. When Mother died, it was that very scripture that I held onto."

"Are you a believer, Rachel?"

"A believer?" she thought for a bit. "I know what Mother taught me."

"That's not what I am asking."

"Then what?"

"Have you ever known God's forgiveness for yourself?"

"Only what Mother has read from scripture."

"So—you do not know of it—for yourself?"

"No, I don't think so," and sensing he was about to tell her, said, "but don't just tell me. I'd rather you show me by scripture how I can do that. I'd have to see it for myself." She looked at him and clasped his arm. "Perhaps, when we get back, you'll show me, won't you, Ransom?"

"Yes, I will. But, Rachel, this is important what I am about to say. Remember when people are mean to you, to forgive them, for God loves them, too."

"I'll try, Ransom." Contentedly, she leaned back against the seat mulling over the things he just told her.

Forgive? I sure need to forgive Pa.

"Ransom?"

"Yes, what is it?"

"Jane and I had a talk last night and I need to ask you something."

He waited for her to continue.

"She said men were after—well—she wouldn't exactly say what they were after. She talked about something called 'one thing'. What was she talking about?"

Ransom sputtered and almost choked on his own saliva as heat started up the back of his neck.

"Ransom?" she asked quizzically, turning to look at him.

Swallowing hard, he wondered just how much he should tell her. If she were not so serious, he would be tempted to laugh out loud.

"Uh...you don't know, Rachel?" he questioned, stifling a grin.

"No." She waited a few moments, then frowning, asked, "Don't you?"

"Well…yes." Wiping his hand across his face, he discovered he had begun to sweat.

"Well?" she asked.

Here goes. Lord, help me through this one.

"Well…it's like what happens between a man and a woman when they get married."

She kept quiet as she waited for him to continue.

I wish she would turn around and look somewhere else at this moment.

Trying his best to sound nonchalant, "And they have a baby."

Turning her head away, she thought about that for a few moments trying to figure out what getting married and having a baby had to do with anything.

"And that's what men are after? Getting married and having a baby?"

"No. No. You've been raised on a farm. You know where newborn calves come from."

"Oh." She studied the road. "I think I understand."

"Why was Jane talking about this, Rachel?"

"Well, she told me that men want women to be helpless, that we have to pretend to be something we aren't. She said those are the kind of women men want to marry."

"What did you say?"

She lifted her chin and said defiantly, "I said, 'then I won't bother to get married'."

Ransom mused over that. "Don't you want children someday?"

She blinked her eyes and pursed her lips. "Well…yes, I guess. I haven't given it much thought, one way or the other.

She cocked her head sideways. "But why should I pretend to be helpless when I'm not? Why can't someone love me the way I am?"

You're more helpless than you realize but I would never tell you that.

"The right man will, Rachel."

"The right man?"

"Yes, the man God has picked out for you. He will love you for what you are…your independence, your character…all that you are."

"Hmm…how will I know the right man?"

"Well, that's between you and God. Study what a godly man is in Scripture. I'll give you some passages to read. God will provide someone who will not only love you, but protect you, too."

"Why can't God love me and protect me?"

"He does. But He created Adam *and* Eve. He enjoys seeing love fulfilled in a godly way through his creation."

She let that sink in for a few moments, then with a smile, said, "He's a wonderful God, isn't He, Ransom?"

"Yes, He is, Rachel."

Rounding the bend that led to home—Rachel began to feel anxious. She leaned hard into Ransom. Without saying a word, he put his arm around her and pulled her close.

CHAPTER TWENTY-FOUR

RACHEL WAS HESITANT TO DISEMBARK from the buggy. Remembering the events that took place here just a few days ago made her feel unsure of herself.

Ransom strode around to the side and with an outstretched hand bade her to step into his arms.

Slowly, she rose and allowed him to help her down. With his arm around her shoulders, she walked to the door, lifted the latch and stepped inside. She crossed to the window, pulled aside the curtains, and opened the shutters, allowing the sunlight to penetrate the semi-darkness of the room as they looked around the cabin.

Ransom noticed the cabin was typical of some who had settled in this area—crude furniture, no stove, but rather a hearth for cooking and heating. Still—a rather tidy place for all its primitiveness. Oddly, a few things stood out in contrast—a few pieces of delicate china, although chipped, an organ, the curtains on the window which were delicate wisps of material, and an exquisite tablecloth draping the crude table as though shielding the table's harshness from inquisitive eyes.

Noticing a miniature portrait on the mantel, he crossed to the hearth and gave a small gasp as he picked it up. The woman in the picture no doubt had good breeding. Her decorum was evident and her clothing the finest he had seen. But it was Rachel's incredible resemblance to her that shocked him.

Rachel was eyeing him intently. Looking up to catch her staring at him, "Your mother?" he asked.

"Yes."

"Lovely!" He marveled as he looked back at the picture. "I can see where you get your beauty."

"You think I look like Mother?"

He raised his head and gazed at her. "Just like her. Beautiful."

"I never thought of myself like that. I could never be like Mother. She was so gentle and always a lady. I don't remember her ever raising her voice to me and she never complained, even when she was sick. So often she'd say, 'Rachel, you're just like your Pa,' and I guess I am," Rachel said, shrugging her shoulders.

She wrinkled her nose as she lifted the lid of her last batch of stew hanging in the hearth. It had molded in the pot, uneaten in her father's hasty retreat.

"I've got to dump this pot—but first, come with me. I want to show you the farm."

Laughing at her impetuosity, he quickly replaced the portrait as she grabbed his arm and began pulling him toward the door.

The way he took nature for granted was completely changed as he looked through Rachel's eyes. She led him from site to site pointing out the different species of plants and trees with their important medicinal uses, and her mother's herb garden that had burst through the earth with the warming of spring. The farm with its springs of water and a deep river that ran along the back edge of the property elicited memories of a joyous childhood and were rehearsed to him through the voice of this young girl who had been encouraged by her father to appreciate its beauty.

He now understood why she longed to be here. She was like a carefree and frolicsome yearling and she totally enchanted his heart.

Drawn into her world, it was easy to relate to and with her. Mesmerized by her freedom of spirit, he wanted to laugh.

Suddenly, he placed his hands on his hips, threw back his head and laughed outrageously, for this was freedom ordained by God. God loved his creation and wanted only total happiness for them. Freedom from pain—freedom from heaviness—a snatch of scripture sprang to his mind.

The garment of praise for the spirit of heaviness.

Rachel laughed with him, reveling in their camaraderie.

The morning passed quickly into afternoon and leading him to her mother's grave, she spoke to her remains as she introduced

Ransom.

"Mother, I know you're in Heaven, but I just wanted you to know...I have a friend with me today. His name is Ransom and he has been very good to me. Pa is gone, Mother, but Ransom said he will take care of me. I know you have no worries in Heaven, but I just wanted you to know. Kisses and I love you," she said and bent to place freshly-picked wildflowers on her grave.

He noticed the afternoon sun was now at its hottest and reluctantly told Rachel they had to collect her things and be going.

Feeling hungry, she asked if they might eat lunch at the "baptizing place" of the river. Though close to town, it seemed nonetheless the perfect ending to such a memorable day.

The lunch she had prepared satisfied the hunger of their stomachs, but another hunger was gnawing at her. While Ransom packed the remains of lunch back into the basket, she slipped away quietly to retrieve something she had brought from the cabin.

"Ransom?"

Looking up from his kneeling position, he noticed her hands were behind her back. "What are you up to now?" he questioned.

She produced her mother's Bible and held it out for him to take. "You promised to show me scriptures on how to make Christ my personal Savior. Remember?"

He took it from her and motioned for her to sit beside him. He opened to Romans 10:8-10, placed the Bible in her lap and told her to read that passage.

"But what saith it? The word is nigh thee, even in thy mouth, and in thy heart: that is, the word of faith, which we preach; That if thou shalt confess with thy mouth the Lord Jesus, and shalt believe in thine heart that God hath raised him from the dead, thou shalt be saved. For with the heart man believeth unto righteousness; and with the mouth confession is made unto salvation."

"Do you understand, Rachel, what you've just read?"

"I think so."

"Then are you ready to become a believer?"

"Yes."

"Rachel, do you repent to God of any sin you have committed in your life?"

"Yes."

"Do you believe that God raised Jesus from the dead?"

"Yes."

"Do you confess him as Lord of your life—that you submit your will to His?"

"Yes."

"Then if you've done these things, by faith you are saved."

Smiling, she said, "Yes, I do repent, I do believe, and by faith I accept Him as Lord.

"Ransom?" her voice questioned as she opened her eyes.

"Is there something else, Rachel?" Ransom asked.

Her eyes fastened on the river. "Will you baptize me, right now?"

He smiled. "I would love to, Rachel. But Father is the pastor of the church and I don't want to overstep his authority."

With an answering smile, she asked, "Then, when he baptizes me, will you come with me in the water?"

Giving her a hug, he said, "You can count on it!"

The neighing of a horse caused Ransom to turn his head in its direction. Sally and Wade were sitting astride their horses.

At their look, the smile slipped from Ransom's face even as his arm slid from Rachel's shoulders.

After Rachel retired that evening, Ransom sat in the library relating the day's events to Jacob.

"Father, Rachel wanted me to baptize her today and I let her know I was deferring to you as you are the pastor."

Jacob nodded for him to continue.

"She wants me to help you with the baptism, but, first, I want to tell you something that has been on my heart a long time. I've felt a call to ministry…but, I didn't want you to think that I was just following the footsteps of you, Will or James. It's something I've felt directly from God and I'd like to help you when you baptize her."

Jacob's face softened. "I've already felt the call of ministry on your life, Ransom. I was just waiting for you to declare it for yourself."

With a sigh of relief, Ransom was thankful this hurdle that he had agonized over for so long, was finally crossed.

The church congregated at the river's edge after service that Sunday, and among them stood Sally Munsen smoldering with barely concealed hate. Jacob and Ransom led Rachel into the water as the congregation sang.

"Rachel, have you accepted the Lord Jesus Christ as Savior into your heart?" Jacob inquired in a loud voice for the congregation to hear.

"I have," she answered, just as loudly.

After raising her from the water, Ransom led her to the shore where Elizabeth tearfully waited, hands outstretched and eager to embrace her.

One by one the congregation conveyed their joy at her decision, offered a handshake or a hug. As Ransom stood by Rachel's side, Sally and Wade approached them with a smile and shook Rachel's hand murmuring appropriate remarks for the occasion.

But looking into Sally's eyes, Ransom saw venom that made him want to shudder.

CHAPTER TWENTY-FIVE

HER LESSONS FOR THE DAY OVER, it was with anticipation that Rachel quickly changed into the pants she had brought with her.

Ransom was gathering wood and tools together for Rachel's first project when Will walked in and asked Ransom to come into the office.

"Right, Will," Ransom answered. Turning to Rachel, "Be right back, Rachel and don't you dare leave this room!" he warned.

Entering the office, Will closed the door behind them as Ransom sat down.

"Say, Ransom! You'd better keep this girl under wraps, for she sure fills out a pair of britches better than any man I've ever seen!"

"Stop it, Will," Ransom spoke sharply. "Don't talk about Rachel like that."

Ransom did not dare admit the same thought had crossed his mind and was, in fact, rather startled by her physical maturity upon his first sight of her in her work outfit. But to hear it coming from Will, it sounded indecent.

Will strolled over to his desk, a thoughtful look on his face.

"Little brother, I was serious when I told you to keep her under wraps. I don't agree with what you're doing and think it's only going to lead to trouble."

"What do you mean?" Ransom asked, immediately on his guard.

"I mean…fur's going to start flying in this town. You've got to keep a level head about you, Ransom. Don't let Rachel get under your skin."

"What makes you think she's getting under my skin?" he asked.

Will sat down on the edge of the desk, one foot on the floor, his other leg dangling over the side. "Look. I know she's a pretty girl and it's noticeable you've been acting differently these last few days, but you can't give in to any whim that she might have. People are going to talk and more than that—the men will start to act ugly and you'll be forced to defend her honor."

Ransom shifted in the chair. "Listen, Will—I know you mean well, but this girl is different than the others. She's not only pretty, but she's smart and she doesn't really care what others say about her."

"She'll begin to care when they tar and feather her," Will said, completely irritated by the situation.

"I'm not only concerned about her...I worry about you, too. You are going to get hurt by this whether you realize it or not.

"Listen, Ransom," Will said softly. "As far as I am personally concerned, I don't care what she does. If she wants to wear trousers and learn a trade, I say let her do it. But you need to rein her in a little. Let her know she can't always do things like this. This town will think she needs to be more ladylike and you're the one to make her see that. You know how the people in this town are. They talk, given provocation or none. They won't tolerate anything different from what they've known. And you know, as well as I, that a woman's good name is of first importance."

Ransom shook his head. "I can't do what you want, Will. It would crush her spirit to mold her into the image of this town and I'm not alone in that opinion. Father agrees with me, also."

"I'm afraid Father's love," Will sighed, "allows him to overlook too much."

Will studied him a bit. It seemed Ransom was romantically involved, from Will's viewpoint, but then you could never tell what Ransom was thinking about as he was prone to introspection.

"Are you in love with Rachel?" Will asked point-blank.

Running his hand through his hair, Ransom scowled, "What makes you think I'm in love with her?"

Will shrugged. "Say it's just a hunch."

"Well, I'm not!" he denied hotly. "I'm just a mentor to Rachel. You know what my plans are, Will. I do not intend for anything to stand in my way, including Rachel. I'm going to the university and that's that," Ransom protested sharply.

Will stood up. His face softened and he laid his hand on Ransom's shoulder.

"Look, little brother. I love you and don't want to see you get hurt. You may deny it, but it seems to me you've fallen head over heels in love with this girl and you're refusing to admit it. Be that as it may, just be careful and keep your wits about you. Don't let Rachel unsettle you," he advised.

Opening the door to the back room, Ransom found Rachel bending over, inspecting a recently finished armchair, her hair falling loosely over her face. She straightened up, brushed back her hair with the back of her hand and looked up with an engaging smile.

Ransom did not return the smile as he wrestled with his thoughts.

Was he becoming entangled in something that would undo all his plans? He hoped not. Was Will right? Was he in love with her, or was it nothing more than friendship? Was God guiding him to be her mentor or was he merely rationalizing his true feelings?

Unsettled? Yes, Will was right about that. She unsettled him to no end. But love? That is an entirely different matter.

"No," he finally surmised. "Will is wrong. I'm not in love with her nor she with me."

Shaking off a sense of foreboding, he gave himself completely to the task at hand of teaching his new apprentice.

CHAPTER TWENTY-SIX

HENRY TAYLOR, one of the church's Council members, stopped at the parsonage to inform Jacob that there was an emergency meeting at church. Refusing to divulge any details, he quickly mounted his horse and rode out. Jacob, stunned momentarily, suspected that it somehow involved Rachel.

Arriving with James at the mill, Jacob cornered Will in the office. Upon hearing his father made an infrequent visit to the mill, Ransom joined them.

"Ransom," he directed, "I want you to send Rachel home."

Will asked, "What's going on, Father?"

"Henry Taylor stopped by the parsonage and said a six o'clock emergency meeting is taking place at church. If Wyatt Munsen is behind this—and I imagine he is—he will try and leave you boys out even though you are Council members. I've got a feeling they're meeting about Rachel spending time here at the mill, among other things."

"Is there anything officially they can do about it, Father?" James queried.

"Not officially, no. But they can sure stir up a lot of trouble among the congregation."

Ransom was quiet. Will tried to warn him, but he refused to listen. Should he renege on his promises to her just to keep down trouble? He felt to blame, allowing her to have her way, wanting to please her. But, on the other hand, she would suffer emotionally if forced to become what the Council may expect from her.

No, whatever it cost him, and sad to say his family as well, he must keep his promises unless ordered by his father to do otherwise. He had to know where his father stood.

Clearing his throat and interrupting their conversation, "Father, I need to know what you want me to do. If you want Rachel to stop coming by the mill—then I'll stand by your decision."

Jacob smiled sympathetically at Ransom.

"Thank you, son, but my decision was made when I gave you permission and I still hold to that decision. Wyatt Munsen has tried to run this Council, and for that matter the church, for several years and it is time I put a stop to it. This matter has only brought his behavior to a head and now is the time to have a showdown. Will and James, I'll need you to back me up."

"You can count on us," they both agreed, nodding their heads.

Jacob looked at Will and stated, "Will, you understand Jane's father Jules is on the Council and may very well side with Wyatt."

Expelling a deep breath, Will answered, "Yes, I thought of that."

"It may cause trouble between you and Jane," Jacob warned.

Standing up, Will walked to the window, and looked out. "That may be, Father, but I'll have to stand for what I think is right."

It was clearer than ever to Ransom that this matter may split, not only the church, but his family as well. Feeling impotent, in the face of the fact that what had started from innocent and magnanimous intentions had now parlayed into strife that could cripple their church, he shoved his fists into his pockets.

"Father, I'm not on the Council," said Ransom, "but I'd like to be there."

Jacob laid his hand on Ransom's shoulder. "I know, son, but, sorry," he explained, "this meeting is for the Council only."

Acting on his own, Wyatt Munsen called the meeting to order causing Jacob's ire to rise from the start.

"Wyatt, I'm pastor here and still the head of this Council. We will follow the rules of protocol for this assembly, and for the recording of the Minutes, I am now officially opening this meeting. I am noting for the record the following persons present: William Templeton, James Templeton, Henry Taylor, Harold Bennett, Lee Hardin, Jack Reynolds, Jules Kennedy, Wyatt Munsen, Gerald Miller, and myself."

He continued. "Since it appears there has come about some business that I have not been made aware of—and since I was informed of this meeting by Henry Taylor—I'll ask you, Henry, to state the business at hand."

Henry's face began to flush at this unexpected request, and he looked to Wyatt for affirmation.

"Jacob, maybe it's best if I state the reason," Wyatt muttered tersely.

Jacob looked Wyatt in the eye and said, "Obviously."

"Now, Jacob," Wyatt laughed sourly, "you surely have some idea why this meeting has been called. It is apparent to the Council, since this Rachel Winslow has come into your household that you've begun to let down some standards this town holds to regarding our womenfolk. A woman spending time at the mill and wearing pants is not acceptable to this Council and it's time you did something about it."

Looking at him long and hard, Jacob said, "Wyatt, I refuse to become a marionette for this Council and have always based my actions as pastor of this church on biblical principles. Where can you show me by Scripture that women should not be at the mill and they can't wear trousers?"

"Jacob, Scripture says that women are not to wear anything that pertaineth to a man!"

"Well…can you all agree with me that in biblical times, no one wore breeches, except the priests under their garments? They all wore robes. God spoke to the prophet Samuel, if you will remember, and said, God doesn't look on the outward appearance but rather the heart."

Jacob spread his hands toward them. "You're making too much out of this, men. Rachel only wears pants while she's learning a trade. She's not flaunting them in public and I've given my permission in this matter. And as far as her 'spending time' at the mill, she's receiving tutoring from Ransom a couple of hours a day."

Snickering maliciously, Wyatt retorted, "Yes, I've heard about this so-called tutoring. Did you know Ransom and Rachel were seen at the river acting inappropriately? I'm warning you, Jacob, this girl is loose as some of those girls—well—you know what I'm talking about."

Gerald Miller suddenly became incensed. With eyes narrowed, he bolted from his chair, leaned over the table, and yelled, "How dare you, Wyatt, question the integrity of a young man like Ransom! I've known this boy all his life and you dare cast a reproach on his character?"

Throwing up his hands in the effort to placate Gerald, Wyatt assumed a more submissive attitude.

"Now, Gerald," said Wyatt, "somehow that doesn't carry a whole lot of weight since I have eyewitnesses."

Gerald glared at Wyatt as he asked, "What eyewitnesses? Who are they?"

"Well…now, I didn't want it to come to this. But, if you must know, it's Wade Bennett and my daughter Sally."

"Sally?" Gerald asked, rolling his eyes, his voice a shade louder. "Wyatt, the whole town knows she's been after Ransom for a long time and he won't have anything to do with her. I saw the way she acted the day of the picnic! Talk about somebody loose! And why was Sally with Wade at the river, Wyatt? Answer me that! Sounds a little suspicious to me!"

"Whoa…Gerald," Wyatt replied defensively, "you can't talk about my Sally that way!"

"I not only can…but I am, Wyatt. You've spoiled that girl for years and since Rachel appeared on the scene, Sally has been consumed with jealousy. No! As far as I'm concerned—I am dismissing your allegations."

The Council members were shocked at the vituperative words Gerald Miller hurled at Wyatt in Ransom's defense. His manner had always been gentle and mild, and they hastily began to rethink their opinion of the facts presented. Could Gerald be right? They knew Sally was spoiled and had Wyatt under her thumb and it was obvious to everyone that her sights had been set on Ransom.

As the change in the Council became more pronounced, Jacob decided to give them a clearer picture of the incident at the river.

"Men, it's true that Ransom and Rachel were at the river. What you may not know it was there she accepted Christ as her Savior. I think it is best if you dismiss any charges you have brought against these two young people and clear their names. I know my Ransom and he would not knowingly do anything that would harm or damage his reputation.

"I believe he holds this girl in the highest regard. Now, what say you? With an uplifted hand signify you absolve these two young people from any charge or fault."

One by one the men lifted their hands in affirmation, some hesitantly, with the exception of, Wyatt Munsen and Jules Kennedy.

"Jules?"

He shook his head and frowned. "I don't know, Jacob. I'm not sure at this point."

Disappointed with Jules, he stated, "So be it. The majority have ruled. All allegations are dropped."

Anxiously awaiting Jacob's return, Ransom secluded himself in the library.

"Ransom?" Jacob gently prodded him awake.

Rousing to sit upright and rubbing his eyes, he said, "I'm sorry, Father. I guess I dozed for a while. How'd the meeting go?"

Jacob sat down on the edge of the desk. "Ransom, there's something I've got to know. You've been acting a little peculiar lately, especially around Rachel. Do you have romantic feelings for her, son?"

Taken aback by his father's direct question, Ransom shifted in the chair.

"I—I don't think so, Father," he answered evasively.

"To be truthful, I do have some feelings for her, but that's all it is. I've got my life all planned out, but I don't see Rachel in those plans. I want a wife who will fit in with the congregation and I don't think Rachel would make an appropriate minister's wife.

"She is of excellent character, but I strongly sense she belongs in a different setting. As you know, Father, my heart is set on coming back here in ministry with you. I'll admit I've found it difficult to reconcile my feelings for her and the lifestyle I feel she belongs in. But you can be assured, I won't mess up my life."

"Well, son, sometimes we think we've got God all figured out. Man has the tendency to cling to what he knows and disregard everything else. It's the opposite with God. We don't always know or see His future will and we must walk by faith, trusting that He's leading our footsteps. When a person gets to my age, they begin to realize we really don't know much at all."

Jacob waved his hand at Ransom's surprised look. "Oh, don't get me wrong. We know Scripture and the doctrine and tenets of the Church. The book of Psalm says: *'His acts He made known unto the children of Israel but, Moses knew His ways'.* We can see the wondrous acts of God but never really know His ways and it's important not to only seek His acts, but to comprehend who He really is. Can you understand that, son?"

"I think so, Father," Ransom replied thoughtfully. "I've never really looked at it in that way, but I do believe I have sought the will of God in my life and I'll continue to do so. Until he tells me otherwise—I just can't make decisions based on my feelings."

"Well, I applaud you for your honesty, Ransom."

"Thanks, Father. By the way, what happened tonight?"

Ransom exploded when Jacob informed him of the lies Sally Munsen told her father.

"You know, Father, when I saw Sally and Wade at Rachel's baptism, I had the feeling something was going to happen…and I don't think it's over yet!"

CHAPTER TWENTY-SEVEN

"DO YOU KNOW WHAT YOU'RE ASKING?" Jane stated emphatically. "Me? Speak to Father about Rachel? No, I won't...and as a matter of fact, I happen to agree with him!" Jane replied with a toss of her head, indignant that Will would try to use her to sway her own father.

"I told Rachel that she shouldn't be going to the mill and it serves her right for all the trouble she's got!"

"Jane, how can you wish trouble on Rachel? This girl has lost her family and needs friends now, not enemies. Try to look at this from Father's perspective. He's not trying to make her fit in but only allowing her to be what she is."

"And just what *is* she, Will?" questioned Jane. "Some girl gadding about at every whim that takes her?"

"Be careful what you say about her, Jane," Will warned. "You just don't understand this girl."

She looked at him thoughtfully and said coldly, "Well...Will, could it be maybe *you've* developed feelings for her? Perhaps, you should tell me just exactly what is going on!"

Will's face went white. He turned angry eyes to her, startling her with their intensity.

"How *dare* you speak to me like that, Jane! I've been faithful to you and tried to please you every way I could, but I refuse to stand here and allow you to throw false allegations in my face. I was not the one who arranged for Rachel to be at the mill, but I'm not going to treat her like dirt just because you've become decidedly jealous. She has no one left in this world and I'm not going to join a lynching mob just because she's different. If you can't understand that...then you don't really know me *or* my family."

After a great deal of arguing which led nowhere, Will grabbed some clothes and informed Jane he would be spending the night elsewhere.

The door slammed behind him. "Going to the parsonage, I suppose," she said aloud to the room, "and where Rachel is."

She'd heard the rumors. A wild, country girl and morally loose, they'd described Rachel, going to the mill and wearing pants. It took less than a week for it to spread through the whole town. She saw the women whispering behind their hands and it stuck in her craw that Will was a party to the whole thing.

Trouble was coming. She sensed it. She had tried to warn Will and Rachel, but nobody listened. Even Ransom, a stickler about things, was taken by the girl.

What was it about Rachel? Why did the Templeton men cater to her?

She crossed the room, looked at the mirror, and patted her smooth cheek. "What's wrong with me? I'm poised and pretty," she said to the mirror's reflection.

Looking at Will's favorite chair, she slumped on the settee. She missed him already.

Tears welled in her eyes and Jane dropped her head in her hands. It hurt that Will chose everyone and everything over her. What would she do now that Will was gone? The thought of packing up and going to her parents crossed her mind. But she was not ready for that. Not just yet.

Stepping into the parlor, Will asked, "Mother, can you put me up in my old room tonight?"

"Uh…yes, Will. What's wrong?" she asked, concerned. "What's happened between you and Jane?"

"I'd really rather not discuss it, Mother. Just a difference of opinion."

Jacob rose from the armchair in which he was sitting and steered William toward the library.

Closing the door, Jacob asked, "What's happened? Does this have anything to do with Rachel?"

Running his hand through his hair and pacing the room, Will replied, "Yes. Can you believe it, Father? Jane thinks I've got feelings for Rachel! I'm not going to give in to her on this. If I do, she will have me jumping through hoops for the rest of my life! For goodness sake, I'm a minister! The furthest thing from my mind is going around looking at other women! Jane's been the only girl for me—and as far as I'm concerned, always will be. But it's more than that, Father—she sides with the people in this town against Rachel. It's got me to thinking—if she's this way about Rachel—how will she react in the future in other situations? Frankly, I'm disappointed in Jane."

Sunday service was an uncomfortable event, to say the least, for the church was now divided. The usual civilities prevailed, but questions lingered in the minds of the congregation as the consequence of gossip and slander. The word of Sally's allegations had spread like fire throughout the church. But Gus and several of the other members realized it was just a lot of gossip and went out of their way to walk over and speak to Rachel, much to the disapproval of the others.

Ransom's once untarnished reputation had come into question in the minds of his peers. This was apparent in church that morning as young men turned away, hands over their mouths masking their snickering smiles. The young ladies looked at Rachel with disdain, raising their eyebrows at one another as they whispered the word, 'fast'.

Sally Munsen and Wade Bennett were an inseparable couple with their heads bent conspiratorially together. Ransom didn't like it and still believed they were up to nothing but trouble.

No one in the Templeton household felt compelled to inform Rachel of the allegations against her and they all insisted on staying close to her in their efforts to shield her from some of the church members' cruel remarks.

Jane entered the sanctuary with her father Jules and her mother Katherine. William had been gone for several nights. In their usual Sunday custom, he, along with James, had taken their place on the pulpit in seating reserved for clergy. He refused to acknowledge Jane was there, avoiding any eye contact with her. She glanced woefully at him and sorrow filled her heart for she did truly love him. She could win back his heart and his respect, she surmised. After all, she was carrying his baby. *Dear God, help us! Restore our marriage!* Her husband had left her, but she knew God had not. Still, the loneliness of their home echoed the longing in her heart for her husband.

The congregation was disbursing after the service and Will debated lingering behind to avoid a confrontation with Jane. *What's wrong with you? You're acting childish trying to avoid your own wife.*

With a stiff nod, Will acknowledged her, "Jane."

Jane was determined that Will would not see the pain she was suffering and put on a cheerful face. "Good morning, Will. Uh…Elizabeth asked if I would join your family for dinner today. Would there be a problem with that?"

Startled by her question, he was momentarily unnerved. Mother hadn't mentioned anything to him. Recovering quickly, he answered, "No, of course not. You know that Father and Mother would always welcome you into their home."

With a flutter of her fan, "Great!" she exclaimed. "See you there about two o'clock."

"Fine." He nodded again, trying his best to sound disinterested despite a skip in his heartbeat. Dear God, how he loved her! He missed being with her and with gut-wrenching control he refrained himself from picking her up in his arms and whisking her away.

Will walked Jane home after dinner and at her invitation to come inside, he stepped in and slumped in his favorite chair with a sigh, guilt mounting in his heart for neglecting his own home.

"How are you feeling, Jane?" he asked with concern.

"Other than the morning nausea, I'm doing fine."

Her pregnancy was not his only concern as the air was heavy with uncertainty between them.

She walked to his chair, her hands twisting, and stood before him.

"When are you coming back home, Will?" she asked.

"I don't know, Jane. You know my stand concerning Ransom and Rachel and I can't pretend that things are right between us. I'm not hypocritical, you know that."

"I'm trying to understand your viewpoint, Will, but I can't be hypocritical either." She raised her chin. "I *do* have a right to my opinions and beliefs."

Will raised his head and looked at her.

"I never thought of it that way. Well…it seems we're at cross purposes." He lowered his head again and slipped into deep thought trying to figure out how to avoid further damage to their marriage.

After some time, he looked up and caught her staring at him with apprehension.

With quiet resignation, he said, "All right, Jane. As your husband, I am required by scripture to take care of you. I'll come back, but this is far from over. I may be head of household, but I can't control what you think or what your religious principles are. I'll…I'll sleep in the other bedchamber."

Jane heart was sinking for this was not what she wanted to hear. He was coming back home all right, but only out of a sense of duty.

She expected him to tell her he had missed her and couldn't live without her. That he loved her as she loved him, the words that any wife wants to hear. She was disappointed but wanted him home in spite of his apathy.

He stayed—but it was a different Will that inhabited their home. Quiet and preoccupied in the coming days, he was indifferent to her and often stayed late at the mill. She became dismayed at the impersonal courtesy he extended toward her and wondered if he cared about anything she did. He was polite and disinterested and his reserve toward her came with an unspoken warning to keep her distance. She missed the old Will with whom she could banter and most of all, she missed the intimacy which they had shared.

Will, on the other hand, had his own struggles. In the darkness of the night, her soft crying tore back the curtain of silence and everything within him wanted to lay aside his principles and go to her.

CHAPTER TWENTY-EIGHT

THERE WAS A CHANGE in the atmosphere at the mill. Where there had been a pleasant camaraderie, there was now unease. Curiosity seekers now gathered there and one in particular, Wade Bennett.

Wade was taking a special interest in Rachel, much to the Ransom's consternation, and had repeatedly asked to walk her home. Ransom became increasingly alarmed at the obvious flattery he was heaping on Rachel, and that she seemed to be succumbing to his attention.

Could he be jealous of Wade? Maybe…but it was more than that. He noticed the leering looks that Wade plainly gave her, as his eyes traveled the length of her. Trying to head off Wade's questionable intentions, Ransom made Rachel leave a little early each day, or stay later and walked her home himself.

"Rachel, I want to talk to you about something," Ransom said late one afternoon as they headed home. "Be careful of the boys that want to walk you home."

"You mean Wade?" She clasped her hands in front of her as she thought of his attentions toward her. "He seems really nice. I think he likes me, Ransom."

"Hmm…well, just be careful. You never know what his intentions are, and I don't think you need to be seeing anyone right now. You're too young."

"Too young?" Her chin rose. "I don't think I'm too young to see someone. Besides, I've got a birthday coming up soon and I'll be sixteen."

"You're young in the sense that you've lived a sheltered life. I'm not sure Wade is the right boy for you. I've got a bad feeling about him."

"Did you know he's asked me to go on a picnic with him?" she asked flippantly.

Suddenly alert, "When did this happen?" Ransom asked.

She kicked at a rock on the road. "A couple of days ago," she finally said. "I told him I'd think about it."

His lips pursed in a hard line. "You can't do this. I'm warning you, Rachel. Stay away from him!"

"Warning me!" she said, suddenly angry. "What gives you the right to tell me what to do?" she cried hotly. "I'll see who I want, Ransom Templeton!"

Grasping her arm and forcing her to stop, he turned her toward him. "You've got to listen to me, Rachel. Wade only wants one thing from you. You don't understand. There's been talk—uh, people will talk. Promise me, you won't go with him," he pleaded.

That silenced her for a moment. True, she had heard gossip swirl around other people in the community, but would anyone truly care about her seeing a gentleman friend? Trying to wrench her arm free from his grasp, "Why should anyone care if I decide to see Wade Bennett?" she asked perversely. "It's none of their business."

"In the first place, people make it their business, I've told you that. And in the second place, you shouldn't go without a chaperon."

"A chaperon? What's a chaperon?"

"A chaperon is someone that protects your reputation by making sure you're not alone with a young man."

"Why do I need a chaperon? I've been alone with you and nobody has said a word."

"That's different," he answered.

"Why is *that* so different?"

"It just is. I'm telling you, Rachel, you can't go!"

Raising her voice, she pulled back from him. "Don't, Ransom. Let me go!" With one wrench she tore herself loose from his arm.

He stopped and she rushed ahead of him. Tensing his jaw and jamming his fists in his pockets, he sensed that he had lost this argument. She was strong-willed and he wondered if they had done right by keeping her in the dark about the town gossip. Maybe it was time to have a talk with Father.

Ransom and Jacob settled in the library after dinner at Ransom's request.

"What's going on, Ransom?"

Ransom stood and began pacing the floor. "It's Rachel, Father. Things have changed at the mill and I don't like what's going on. Some of our church people are becoming noticeably un-Christ-like."

"I know," he agreed with a nod of his head.

"Wade Bennett is spending time at the mill, trying to consort with Rachel. I don't feel his intentions are good, Father. He is leering at her and she innocently thinks his interest in her is above suspicion. Is it best to keep Rachel in the dark about all this?"

Running his fingers through his hair, he continued, "I never dreamed the ungodliness of this town would rear itself in an ugly way like this. She's so innocent and has no idea of the storm that's brewing."

"Gossip is like mud on a shirt, Ransom," said Jacob. "You can wipe it off, but it still leaves a stain. Often people want to believe the worst about others because of their own innate unrighteousness. Listen, son, you have assumed a lot of responsibility for Rachel and your mother and I are grateful. I've allowed you free rein with her because she seems to relate more easily to a young person like you than she does me or Elizabeth. If you want her to quit going to the mill, then I'll go along with your decision."

Ransom rubbed his forehead. "That won't work, Father. She won't understand."

"Whew!" Jacob exclaimed. "It's time I took the responsibility here instead of burdening you. Elizabeth and I will have a talk with her this evening. I'll try not to clip her wings—but she needs to understand the precautions she needs to take. I think now's the time to let her know a few things."

CHAPTER TWENTY-NINE

"DID YOU TALK WITH FATHER AND MOTHER LAST NIGHT?" Ransom asked as he absently picked through the lunch that Rachel had brought to the mill.

"Yes, and I saw Wade on my way over and told him I would not go with him," she answered meekly.

Hearing this uncharacteristic submissive tone in her voice, he looked at her and chuckled, "Good."

Wade did not show up at the mill that day as he usually did. "I guess Rachel put him in his place," Ransom thought.

Will had left early that day leaving Ransom to stay until closing time.

"There's still another hour before we close, so you go on home," he told Rachel, feeling at ease because Wade had not appeared and all the men had gone for the day.

Glancing over an order that needed to be filled and feeling cheered that things were back to normal, he threw himself into the task at hand.

As he worked, suddenly, a strong sense of urgency to leave the building possessed him. Trying to shrug it off, it grew stronger until he finally prayed, *Lord, is there something wrong?*

Locking up as quickly as he could, he rushed out, feeling driven by a power greater than himself. Before he had reached the edge of town, a cry for help reached his ears and sent shivers down his spine. It was coming from the direction of an abandoned building once lived in by the Welling family. Tall weeds had overgrown the path leading to the door. Wade Bennett's horse, barely visible, was tied to the maple sapling in the side yard.

A light shower had passed through Wellington earlier and running through the wet weeds toward the direction of the cries,

Ransom reached the dilapidated building. The decayed door barely hung on its hinges and with a shove he dislodged it, sending pieces of rotting wood hurling across the floor. Once inside, his eyes had difficulty adjusting to the semi-darkness. A movement near the stone hearth drew his attention and he saw a flurry of skirts pushed up toward the waist of a woman struggling beneath a man whose trousers had been loosened.

"What's going on here?" Ransom shouted. The attacker in his frenzied passion had not heard the clatter of wood hitting the floor…or realized Ransom was there. Startled, he turned his head and with glazed eyes stared up at Ransom without relinquishing his hold as he kept the woman pinned to the floor. Ransom was so horrified that the breath went out of his lungs with a gasp. Wade Bennett was forcing himself upon the woman.

"Ransom! Help me…help me!" cried the distraught girl. In shock, he recognized the voice. It was Rachel!

"Stay out of this, Ransom. She deserves this!" Wade spat at him.

Ransom looked at Wade as though he had not even spoken. Rachel, twisting and crying, trying to escape the weight upon her, let out a blood-curdling yell.

Ransom was not a fighting man. He had never been as he was prone to be long-suffering. But a sudden, blinding, fury enveloped him, and he pulled Wade off Rachel with a strength fueled by rage and flung him across the room. Then he pulled Wade to his feet and swung blow after fisted blow. Knocked to the floor and then hoisted up again time after time to endure Ransom's hits, with a final thud, Wade finally fell and lay moaning in a bloody pool.

His anger spent…Ransom dazedly stretched forth blood-covered hands that looked unfamiliar to him. These were not the hands of ministry. His temper waning now, Ransom became sick with revulsion at what had just happened.

Reprieved by Ransom's stunned reaction, Wade crawled to the threshold of the door. Laboriously, he pulled himself up, fumbling with his trousers, fearing another attack. Stumbling across the overgrown lawn, he fell. Crawling until he finally reached his horse, with the last ounce of strength he could muster, he pulled himself up to finally slump in the saddle. Weary and injured, Wade rode away.

Tears of fright and hysteria streamed down Rachel's face and as Ransom started toward her, she instinctively recoiled and cried, "Stay away!"

Heart in his throat, Ransom stopped. Reaching out to her, he wanted to take her in his arms and console her, but she wanted no part of him.

"I have only myself to blame," Ransom muttered under his breath. Time and again he had witnessed Sally and Wade together and sensed they were contemplating foul play. Hoping against hope that things would turn out for the best, he had ignored what he had felt.

And the result of his turning a blind eye was rape. Rape! How would Rachel ever get over this?

Ransom turned from Rachel and his tall body stood in the door-less frame, looking again at his bloodied hands, turning them over slowly, looking at the palms and then the backs as though he never seen them before.

In a sudden moment of self-knowledge that turned quickly to self-loathing, he realized a dark side of himself that was capable of murder. The revelation frightened him. So proud he had been to be an epitome of all that was godly. Now he realized how thin the line was between good and evil, and how easily it could be crossed. That knowledge shook him to the core.

Reaching down, he fingered his shirt. It had been wrenched from his trousers and torn as Wade clutched it in a desperate attempt to keep himself on his feet.

It's completely my fault, thought Ransom dully as he looked at Rachel. Father tried to warn me. So had Will and James. "Will!" he groaned aloud. How can I face him now? The last thing I need to hear is how right he was and how wrong I've been! He was right. This is my fault. I knew better.

Why didn't I listen to him! In spite of their warnings, I've lived an illusion. Nothing could ever happen to us, I thought. Not the Templeton family! It was I who insisted that Rachel have her head about things…whatever she desired to do.

And now look at what's happened! She's violated! I've lived my whole life by the conventions of society! This dark-eyed beauty comes into my life and I sweep all my principles aside, thinking everyone understood her as I did! What a rude awakening!

It was a long time before she calmed down enough for him to get her home.

She begged Ransom to take her to the farm. She didn't want to face anyone now, maybe never.

Everything within him wanted to take her there, there where she would feel safe. He knew running away wouldn't solve the problem, but just what the solution was he didn't know.

He needed Father to tell him what to do.

A gnawing worry grew as he wondered what story Wade would tell…if any at all. Surely, he wasn't such a fool as to tell the town what he had done. Would he brag or be shamed into silence?

CHAPTER THIRTY

OH! THEY HAD WARNED ME, all of them, Rachel thought grimly. Warned me to be careful.

But she had scoffed at their admonitions. Why hadn't she listened? Determined that they wouldn't change her to become like one of them, she had brought this on herself.

What would she do? Where would she go? If she thought she was an outcast before, that paled in comparison to what awaited her now. She would be regarded as no better than a harlot.

Beginning to panic, Rachel envisioned long years of open rejection, women whispering behind their fans while men snickered. The thought of it was more than she could bear. She began to shake uncontrollably.

Rachel pressed her hands to her forehead and ran her fingers through her hair. She realized her hair had loosened from the egrettes. Scrambling in the near darkness, her hands frantically searched for them, sifting through rubbish left behind by vagrants. Over and over the scene replayed in her mind as she looked.

But she needed them, needed something of beauty to quell the mounting sense of violation and storm of self-loathing. Something beautiful, that would distance her from this ugly, sordid ordeal. Finding the egrettes and frantically brushing away the dirt, with shaking hands and chattering teeth, she tried desperately to pin them into her tangled hair.

It was now dusk and to avoid the stares of anyone that might be out at that time, Ransom led her through the darkened woods that encircled the town until they reached the back door of the parsonage, where they were met by Will and Jane.

Noticing Rachel's dishabille and the blood splattered on Ransom's shirt and hands, Will and Jane unleashed a flurry of concerned questions.

"What in the world happened to you two? Where have you been? It's after nine o'clock. Mother and Father are out looking for you!"

In a broken voice, Ransom described the attack that had taken place, carefully avoiding the word 'rape'.

"Oh! You poor thing!" Jane uttered compassionately as she rushed to embrace Rachel.

Jacob, Elizabeth, and James walked in as Rachel burst into renewed tears.

Nearly fainting from the scene that she had walked into—bloodied shirt and incoherent crying, Elizabeth was immediately up in arms as Ransom once more unfolded the crisis they had just been through.

"Jacob, send immediately for Harold and Beatrice Bennett," Elizabeth indignantly demanded. "Never has anything like this happened in Wellington and Wade needs to be prosecuted for it!"

Sensing the situation was spiraling out of control, Jacob suggested that Elizabeth and Jane take Rachel upstairs.

"What are you going to do, Father?" James asked.

Passing his hand over his face, he replied, "We need to think this through. Since you and Will are on the Council, we should decide some course of action before this goes any further.

"On the one hand, Wade should be disciplined by the Council and prosecuted by law. On the other hand, when word gets out about this, the church will be ripped apart and, we will all be blamed, including Rachel. She will be tainted in their eyes and will never live it down. I think for right now, it's best to meet with Wade himself and then decide what action to take. Rather than raise any suspicion for the present, I want you, Will, to bring Wade to my church office tomorrow morning. Ransom, stay home tomorrow and James can take your place at the mill."

They were interrupted by a knock on the door. James rose to answer it and was met by ashen- faced Harold Bennett. Pushing past James, Harold entered the parlor and crossing to Jacob, grabbed his arms, tears streaming down his face.

"Jacob! It's Wade. His horse threw him—broke his neck—he's dead! You've got to come! Beatrice is nearly out of her mind!"

As a stunned look passed between Jacob and his sons, he finally answered, "Of course, Harold. I'll be there in a few moments. Just let me take care of a couple of things first."

Harold nodded and left as quickly as he came.

Alone in the library, Ransom told Jacob what he dreaded to reveal. "I prefer you keep this in confidence, Father," he prefaced.

In response to Jacob's questioning look, he continued. "It was more than just an attack. Rachel was raped."

In Will's eyes, Jane's fury had gone a long way toward undoing the emotional separation that had divided their marriage. Arriving home in the wee hours of the morning, Jane was still fuming.

"I know I didn't agree with your family initially, but this town's ugliness has gone too far. When they can gossip and influence our young people into something like this, it is downright poisonous. I won't stand for it, even if it means disagreeing with my father. No one has the right to commit such acts even if they feel they are deserved. It's going to take Rachel a long time to get over this, if she ever does.

"Oh, Will! I'm so sorry. Rachel is the innocent victim in all of this. Forgive me for being such a fool."

Without saying a word, he took her into his arms.

It was not an easy funeral for Jacob to preside over. No one in town knew what had taken place in the few hours before Wade's accident and Jacob decided it best that it be kept confidential.

Ransom felt something akin to self-loathing as Wade lay in the casket. His stomach soured as the events replayed over and over in his mind. He had always prided himself on his self-control and the startling realization that he in fury could have killed a man made him unsure of himself.

Pride goeth before a fall. Prideful, that's what he had been, secure in his own self- righteousness and his own spiritual strength. How quickly one could fall, and the thought filled him with fear!

Standing in front of Wade's casket, Sally moaned inwardly. I never meant for it to come to this. I am to blame for his death. Wade loved me…I know he did. I pushed him to do the hideous things he did. He only acted at my urgings and now he's gone.

Looking at Ransom sitting in the pew, she now realized there would never be anything but friendship between them. As he caught her glance, she tried to convey her regret in her eyes, but he looked away. She wished, in that moment, that she could unburden herself to all that were gathered there but lacked the courage. This was something she would bitterly take to her grave.

CHAPTER THIRTY-ONE

THOUGH SHE RECOVERED PHYSICALLY from Wade Bennett's rape, mentally, Rachel was dazed and ill. Always before, she'd rebounded quickly from any setback that life had hurled at her. Where she had been unafraid of anything before, now, she became filled with fear at the nearness and strength of a man.

She had always found her father's physical strength a comfort and something she had depended on, but a man's strength now loomed as an enemy in her mind, highlighting a woman's relative weakness. Not that she thought of her father as a villain…to her he was not like the others.

"Pa, I need you!" her heart cried out. She no longer felt safe and every shadow cast a dark fear of injury over her. Night after night she would awaken in terror and revulsion, alarmed by her nightmarish dreams.

Rachel had grown uncharacteristically withdrawn. She rarely smiled and spoke only when spoken to. Doctor Stone was called in and the tonics he gave her failed to remedy her ever-present anxiety and despondency.

In a frantic attempt to keep her mind occupied, Elizabeth had Jane and Cissa over often and they plied her with activity such as learning to cook and sew.

The wedding was approaching and putting the finishing touches on Rachel's dress brought no joy to her. As she tried on the dress, Cissa complimented her, saying the dress made her look beautiful. But when Rachel looked in the mirror at herself, she saw only defilement.

Ransom's eyes followed her constantly, looking for some sign—any sign, that things between them could be as they once were. She distanced herself from him, not that she meant to hurt him, but the demons that plucked at her mind made her cringe at the thought of physical contact with him or any man, for that matter.

She refused to go to the mill and when he suggested doing her studies at home, she always had an excuse ready.

Ransom was in a continual state of worry and he took no pains to hide it. Rachel ate very little and as her cheekbones became prominent, he grew distraught. He tried to reach out to her, but the wall she ensconced herself behind yielded no crack that he might chip away.

Often at night he heard her cry out in her sleep, but she kept her door locked. Ransom was at a loss and the wisdom his father often attributed to him now seemed elusive. His protective force that, in the past, had kept Rachel's heart open, freeing her from hurt, now became a grim reminder of Wade's violation, and kept her away from Ransom's healing touch.

A couple of weeks had passed. It was later than usual one evening when Ransom walked through the back door looking haggard. It had been a rough day at the mill and he hadn't been sleeping much. He'd missed dinner and decided to warm the leftovers himself. Standing at the stove, he felt, rather than heard, someone behind him. Turning quickly, he saw Rachel about to escape from the room.

"Here, Rachel. Warm my food for me, won't you? I'm bone-tired and need to sit down." He held the spoon out to her and after some hesitation she walked toward him and took the spoon. He sank into a kitchen chair and propping his elbows on the table and putting his head in his hands, almost immediately fell into a light sleep.

She heard his slight snoring behind her and turned to look at him. Her heart constricted as she saw a lock of auburn hair fall over his forehead. He had been worried about her...she knew that. Hadn't been sleeping much either. Often when she woke from her terrifying dreams, he was there knocking on her door, but she purposely had kept him locked out.

She hated to wake him now when he so desperately needed to sleep. But he needed to eat. She was careful to place the plate on the table out of his reach, lest he wake and send it crashing to the floor. With her hand on his shoulder, she gave him a slight shake. "Your dinner's ready," she said quietly.

He rubbed his eyes and looking at the plate, reached out to pull it to him.

"Thanks," he said gratefully.

She started to leave, "Don't leave," he entreated her, "Stay with me."

She looked into his tired eyes.

"Please?" he asked with a touch of a smile at the corners of his mouth.

Taking a seat across the table, she watched as he ate. His face was inscrutable as he attempted conversation. Impersonal business talk…that was all.

Will had started construction on his store, did she know that? They were working hard to turn out enough furniture to give it a good grand opening. Will was thinking about adding dry goods.

"Will is a good businessman, always did have a good head about him," Ransom remarked.

"When did Ransom get those dark circles under his eyes?" she asked herself. "Oh, how tired he looks. I've been so engrossed in my own problems that I haven't paid much attention to him."

Shamed, she felt a sudden flash of sympathy. Wanting somehow to reach out to him and take the exhaustion from him, she considered the goodness he'd shown toward her through everything.

Ransom finally swallowed the last bite and downed his drink.

He rose, scraping back his chair and wavered slightly. "Thanks for the company," he said and headed for bed.

As the days passed, Ransom faced the reality that he was more than a mentor to Rachel. He, in fact, loved her.

Reflecting on what Gus had said, he had to concede that on that first eventful day, he had indeed fallen in love at first sight. Hard as he had fought those feelings, they were a part of his being, as sure as he breathed and something he now wholeheartedly accepted.

Looking at her, he knew the fact that she had been raped would bother most men.

But not him.

He loved her as much, if not more, than ever. If only—he could let her know.

CHAPTER THIRTY-TWO

THE DAY OF THE WEDDING HAD FINALLY ARRIVED. It was unusually hot for the first weekend in July. It was sweltering, causing Cissa, in hindsight, to wish she had set an earlier date. Because Rachel had never seen a wedding take place, as promised, they agreed to meet at the church the night before to rehearse.

Rachel had pleaded with Jacob and Elizabeth to excuse her from being a part of the wedding party. She did not feel she could face a crowd of people. Elizabeth desperately wanted to accommodate her, but Jacob refused.

"How can you be so hard-hearted? Elizabeth said. "You know what Rachel has been through."

"Rachel can't run from life. As hard as it might be, she has to adjust," he said. Jacob explained to both the responsibility of keeping her commitment to James and Cissa, for they had stood with her in tough times. "This is one of the happiest days of their lives and it's important not to ruin it with personal problems," Jacob counseled.

Rachel was struggling. How could she go on like this? Even as she pondered her situation, she knew Jacob was right and that some attempt had to be made at normalcy or she was lost.

Why should she let Wade Bennett, now dead, control her from the grave? As hard as it might be, no matter how many demons she had to fight, she just had to get on with life, as Jacob said.

After all, look what I've come through so far. Yes, James and Cissa have been good to me. They've all been good to me, she thought. What could she give them in return? She had no gift to bring other than herself. Yes...she felt good about that. Her gift would be to make sure their special day would only be happy memories. If she had to fight back her own bad memories for the rest of the day, that is what she would do.

Walking down the aisle in rehearsal, Rachel looked at the face of Ransom as he waited for her. Her heart contracted at the tortured look in his eyes as they scanned her face, looking for release from the prison in which he was bound.

Coming forward to meet her, careful not to make any sudden movement, he stopped, heedless of any other person in the room. Holding his breath and slowly extending his arm for her to take, his eyes remained riveted upon her.

For a timeless moment, she stood there staring at him. Then after a low sigh, her eyes softened, and her lips flickered in a near smile as she rested her fingertips upon his arm and he escorted her in position.

To the family that was watching spell-bound, if Rachel was not in love with Ransom, it was obvious that he was deeply in love with her.

The reception was like a soothing balm to Ransom. Rachel was more like her old self as she became the center of attention among the young people. The girls complimented her dress and her hair which had been done up by Jane.

As the small band of musicians began to play, Ransom whisked her away from the approaching young men and steered her toward the temporary dance floor built for the reception.

They were playing an allemande.

"Come on, Rachel, let's dance."

"I can't, Ransom," she replied with a shake of her head.

"Why not?" he asked as a furrow formed in his brow.

"I don't know how," she admitted.

He had forgotten there were so many things she didn't know about.

"Well, come on, anyway. I'll show you how. You just follow my lead," he said and flashed a smile.

"All right. But don't blame me if you end up with sore feet!" she challenged.

They joined the line of couples. Rachel tried to follow but couldn't master the dance. She was making a spectacle of herself as she broke the rhythm of the dance, so she pulled away from him in frustration and stomped off the floor.

Grabbing her arm, he said, "Wait…listen. Let's try this again."

He turned and looked at a grove of trees.

With a mischievous smile, he urged, "Come on."

He hurriedly pulled her out of sight of the others into a shaded glade as the music from a distance carried its melodic strains through the air.

A waltz had started. "If I'm going to teach you how to dance, I'll have to hold you a little closer."

She nodded to him as he sought her permission.

She allowed his arm to encircle her waist as he clasped her hand and pulled her closer to him. He whirled her around in dizzying turns and she fell in step.

Excited that she was actually dancing, she reminisced to Ransom of her mother's ability to play the organ. There had been music at home, but no dancing.

As he drew her closer, her words became lost in his heart's longing. It seemed so long since he had enjoyed the pleasure of her touch and now holding her in his arms, he was nearing the danger point of spilling his love for her. He could smell the cologne in her hair and her nearness was stirring up his pent-up emotions.

Hardly aware that he was moving, he slowed his pace until he finally stopped. Rachel looked up at him questioningly.

For what seemed an eternity, he stood there drowning in the pool of her dark eyes and the thudding of his heart quickened. His hand moved to trace the contour of her face as he quietly whispered her name and slowly bent to kiss her.

As visions of Wade Bennett swam before her eyes, she pulled away with a sharp, resounding, "No!" Stepping back and pointing her finger at him, "No! No! No!" she reiterated. Then she turned and ran, stumbling from the church grounds without any thought of where she was headed.

Like cold water dashed upon him, came the realization of what he had done. He knew what she had been through, her torturous nightmares. She had closed her heart from him once and now he had driven her away again.

Cold sanity now took control over hot passion. She trusted him and dared to allow him into her world again and he betrayed her! He had to convince her that he meant her no harm. He would never treat her as Wade had done.

"You fool! She doesn't know that," he said out loud.

Stepping from the glade, he looked in all directions. Where would she have run to?

Reaching the parsonage and checking the house, he discovered she had not come there.

"Think, Ransom, think! Where would she go?" he said to himself, reason trying to break through frantic worry. There were only two places he thought she might go. Her farm or—yes, that's it—the river!

He was so agitated that his fingers fumbled at his attempt to saddle his horse, but he finally mounted and rode to the outskirts of town. Turning off the road and riding through the thicket of woods, with relief, he finally spotted Rachel as he reached the opening to the river.

Sitting astride his horse, he watched as she lay at the river's edge. She was so still that he felt a frisson of unease. Is she all right? Alighting, he quickly made his way through the clearing toward her, fearing the worst.

Hearing footsteps coming toward her, she pushed herself up from the ground and, turning with fear on her face, saw it was Ransom.

She's all right, he kept thinking as he advanced toward her, his relief at finding her safe.

She was about to run again when he called, "Rachel!" and halted his steps.

He extended his hand to her. "Rachel, please! Let me talk to you.

I—I promise I won't hurt you. Rachel, please, don't shut me out. Just let me talk. I—I won't touch you."

She sat down on the rocks and put her face in her hands, trembling and exhausted by her run to the river. She thought she had her nightmarish thoughts under control but found she was still tormented by them. Would she never get over this? Would this haunt her for the rest of her life? What could he possibly do or say that would deliver her from this torment she was in? Where was the strength that she had so proudly declared she possessed?

With a pleading note in his voice, Ransom advanced slowly toward her, murmuring words that endeavored to convince her to trust him. She raised her head and watched as he stepped to the river's edge, keeping a safe distance from her.

His words went on softly in the glare of the hot summer afternoon and the sticky stillness was unbearable as the sun drew salty sweat to the surface of her body. His voice began to fade away until…finally…there was the blackness of nothingness.

Coming slowly back to consciousness, too numb for emotion, she realized she was lying under the shade of the trees with her head in white-faced Ransom's lap. She was weary. She had tried to be strong but had failed miserably.

He was watching her intently with an anxious look on his face. Struggling, she tried to rise, but he refused to let her up.

"Lay there until you get your strength back," he said, sounding more like the old Ransom giving her orders.

Strange, that that tone of his voice was just what she needed. She started to smile but the smile died before it reached the corners of her mouth.

He gave her a thoughtful look and decided it was time to take the situation in hand.

"You may not want to hear what I have to say, but you're going to listen to me, Rachel."

She roused at his challenge and sat up.

Noting her drawn eyebrows and the stubborn look in her eyes, he pressed on.

"I know you've been through a lot and I'm not underplaying that...but you've made me about crazy. You shut me out when I've only had the best intentions toward you. I've been worried sick about you, and it hurt me to know when I reached out to you, that my touch only repulsed you. I know I got carried away a while ago, but I care about you a great deal. I realize you're hurting, but it's time you understood. I've suffered also. I can't go through this anymore—and if you won't let me help you—"

"I have something to say, Ransom," she broke in. As he tried to continue, she stilled him by pressing her hand over his mouth. "No, don't interrupt me." Removing her hand, she moved away from him a little. "There's something I need to tell you."

He lay back, propping himself against the tree, watching her.

She drew in a deep breath. "I know I've hurt you by drawing away from you in these past few weeks. What you need to understand is—it's not you—er—men that I've become afraid of, it's their physical strength. I don't know if you can understand that. When—when Wade overpowered me—I became aware of my own bodily weakness and felt vulnerable. I had always felt so strong, able to take care of myself. I guess it is always a shock when you discover a weakness in yourself and especially when it leads to tragedy."

Giving him a smile, she continued, "I think a lot of you, Ransom, and appreciate all you've done for me. I've never thanked you for rescuing me from Wade and I want you to know I'm grateful. You've been a good friend to me. I—I just needed some time to come to terms with all this."

She paused. "Does any of this make any sense to you?"

He had not understood what was driving her to act the way she did toward him, he saw that now. He had to admit she was smart to figure this out by herself. He thought of Wade and his own feeling of vulnerability after he brutally attacked him in Rachel's defense.

"Yes, I think I do, Rachel," he replied. He paused thoughtfully for a moment.

Choosing his words carefully, he went on, "I'd always been so proud of my self-control. When I saw Wade lying in his own blood after I beat him…I was shocked that I could have been so violent. Frankly, the fact that I allowed anger to rule, shook me. I'd always felt confident of my willpower. Realizing that in a moment's time my restraint could be tossed overboard made me question my Christianity.

"I—I just want you to know, I wouldn't hurt you for anything, Rachel."

Thinking on his answer, "I know you wouldn't," she said, leaning back against the tree beside him. "I just want you to know it wasn't you I was running away from. It was Wade."

Sitting beside her, Ransom suddenly felt inclined to take her hand, but refrained from doing so. He did not want to leave her but, soon, he would ride for the university. She needed him, though she did not know it.

"I'm leaving soon, Rachel," he informed her.

She nodded. "Yes, I know."

"I won't be back until spring."

She whispered "Oh," then grew still. She had not realized he would be away that long.

He did not want to leave her and nearly told her so but he had no right. His plans came first. Still—he did not want to leave.

"Will—will you manage after I'm gone?" he said, instead.

With a grunted laugh, she said, "You know me, Ransom. I always come through."

He smiled. She did, indeed.

"You're my one true friend, Ransom."

She turned to him. "Do you mind if I come back to the mill?"

A look of relief swept over his face. "Mind? I'd be disappointed if you didn't."

CHAPTER THIRTY-THREE

WILL HAD HIS FURNITURE STORE OPENED BY THE LAST OF JULY. He followed through on his idea of adding dry goods to his inventory to draw the ladies in, hoping this would encourage their husbands to purchase his furniture as they shopped.

It was all he could do to keep his mother from working in the store. He had convinced her that she was too busy in his father's ministry.

"Better yet," he thought, "Rachel and Cissa could work there and between Ransom, James, and himself they could take turns overseeing the store."

Perfect solution. It got Rachel out of the mill. Maybe the town would settle down and quit giving her such a hard time.

Surprisingly, Ransom was the one who objected. With her gone from the mill, he was pining away, acting like one who was lovesick.

"Ridiculous," Will thought. "He sees her every morning and evening."

"Ransom, you mess up one more order and I'm going to kick you out of here," Will growled as he inspected the order Ransom had just filled.

"Sorry, Will. I don't know what's wrong with me," he lamented as he threw up his hands. "You know I've always done a good job."

Will shifted some lumber to another pile. "I know what's wrong with you. You're thinking about that girl! I wish you'd make up your mind one way or another about her and get on with your life."

He nodded in agreement. "Yes, I know you're right. But, confidentially, Will, I don't know what her feelings are toward me."

Will looked up from his bent-over position. "Well, how is she going to have any feelings if you don't at least try to court her? Honestly, you treat her like a sister when everyone knows you're in love with her. Everyone, that is, except Rachel."

"I've told you my stand on that, Will. I'm not sure she'll fit in with the ministry I have in mind, so I'm not going to lead her on."

Will rolled his eyes as he straightened and stretched his back. "Well, remember, he who hesitates loses. If you are not careful, someone will come along and sweep her off her feet and *then* where will you be? Standing by the side of the road crying, *that's* where you'll be."

"I'm still praying about it." Ransom said defensively.

"Pray all you want. It's none of my business," Will said. "But I do know what my business is—and that's to keep my mill successful. I want you to knock off at noon here every day and go to the store. Start tutoring her again. That'll give you an excuse to be there. James can work here in the afternoon. Maybe *he* can get these orders right!"

Gratefully, he said, "Thanks, Will."

Rachel looked up in surprise as Ransom walked in at a little after the noon hour.

"What are you doing here?" she asked.

With a grin on his face, he told her, "I'm here to tutor you."

Skeptically, Cissa eyed him. "You don't look like you've got tutoring on your mind to me."

With a deep, sweeping bow, he chortled, "Believe me, dear lady, I have come to rescue this fair damsel from the tedious work of making a living so that she might be subjected to my delightful charms as I enlighten her to the merits of ciphering and grammar."

Cissa and Rachel looked at each other and began to laugh.

"What's put you in this crazy mood today?" Cissa said, still laughing.

His eyes were dancing. "Oh, I just like being around the ladies."

"Hmm…so I see," she retorted thoughtfully. "Might as well go on to the back room then and if you haven't had lunch, there's some left for you." The bell at the door sounded, signaling an arriving customer.

"Thanks," he said as he flashed a grin.

Ransom watched as Rachel took the basket off the shelf and began to unpack the remains of the lunch.

"Sorry, we don't have any milk. You'll have to settle for water," she informed him as she poured from the pitcher into a mug.

When he did not answer, she turned and looked at him quizzically. He refused to drop his gaze and she saw something flicker in his eyes.

Embarrassed, she dropped her eyes and said, "You're acting strange today."

"Am I? How so?" he questioned as he leaned closer.

"I don't know." She handed him the mug. "Usually, you're so serious." She looked into his eyes. "I'm not sure how to take you."

With a mischievous look, "Maybe I don't know how to take myself," he quipped.

She stared at him. "That's silly! Why wouldn't anyone know something like that?"

"Like what?" he said, leading her on.

"You know—" she floundered, tried to concentrate on the food and gave a slight shake of her head. "You're getting me confused today."

He leaned closer and said softly, "Maybe I'm just trying to sort some things out myself."

"What things?" she asked, looking into his eyes, forgetting the food that was in her hand. He was so close to her she was finding it difficult to breathe.

Taking the bread and meat from her, he answered evasively. "Oh…just things." He gave a short laugh. "I've got an idea. Let's go fishing."

"Fishing!" She backed away from him. "Will will have a fit. Besides, you're supposed to be working."

"I'm supposed to be tutoring you, too. How about I tutor you at the river?"

"He's expecting me to help run the store. You'll end up getting me in trouble."

"I'll square it with him." Taking a large bite of the bread he pulled her arm impatiently. "Come on."

Laughing, she said, "Don't you think you'd better bring some writing materials if you're going to tutor me?"

"Oh, of course." he said, giving her a lopsided grin and grabbing the foolscap and inkpot from the desk.

As they left the store, Ransom gave Cissa a wave, announcing they would return later, and left her standing with her mouth open.

For the second week of August, it was cooler than normal. They were sitting at the edge of the clearing under the trees. A slight breeze had kicked up, tossing Rachel's hair across her face, and as she lifted her hand to sweep her locks back, it brushed against Ransom's hand that had risen to do the same. When she glanced at him, there was a certain look in his eyes.

"I thought you were going to tutor me today," she asked.

"I am…I am. I just want to relax a while and enjoy the scenery."

She lay down and, in a very unladylike way, rolled over on her stomach and rose on her elbows. "Yes. It is beautiful here," she murmured as she looked around.

I mean you.

"Rachel, I'm leaving the end of next week," he said.

She picked a wildflower growing there and methodically began plucking its petals. "Yes, I know." Pausing, she then said, "I'll be sad to see you go."

Drawing in a sharp breath, "You will?" he asked.

Rolling to her back, her hair fanned out and she looked up at him. "Yes. You've been a good friend to me, Ransom. You've helped me through these past months, and I want you to know, I sincerely appreciate it. I shall always have fond memories of you."

"Oh," he said, "just fondness," his words thick with disappointment.

"Have I said something wrong?" she asked, a note of concern in her voice.

"No, of course not." He shrugged. "Forget it. Sit up and open your book."

CHAPTER THIRTY-FOUR

IT WAS SATURDAY AND RACHEL'S BIRTHDAY arrived unheralded by any well- wishing at breakfast. She had lain awake during the night almost giggling with anticipation. What gifts might the family shower her with? She'd had her eye on a tawny mare at Gus's livery stable and had actually hinted about it a time or two to Jacob and Elizabeth. When she and Ransom had been to the livery, he had agreed the mare would be perfect for her. "It's a little extravagant," she thought as she bit her lip. "They've always given me what I've asked for. Still…."

Her disappointment grew into petulance and propping her elbows on the table she put her chin in the palms of her hands. "Surely, the most important year of my life would be remembered by someone. Even Ransom, who knows everything about me, hasn't said a word. After all, it *is* my sixteenth birthday and, by some standards, on this day I become a woman."

The house had been silent all morning. Ransom left right after breakfast. Even Elizabeth was gone, making the weekly rounds with Jacob to those who were sick and shut in. She wandered around the rooms picking up and listlessly fondling Elizabeth's treasured bric-a-brac.

Memories of the farm were crowding her mind.

Becoming restless, she decided to go to the livery and convince Gus to loan her the mare. "I just need to take a ride and get away for a while," she told herself.

Gus had just pulled the saddle off a horse when Rachel walked in. He was surprised to see her alone, for rarely was she out of the company of the Templeton family.

"Hello, Rachel. By yourself today?"

"Everyone is busy," she told him forlornly as she stroked the mare's mane. "Today's my sixteenth birthday and nobody remembered."

"Well, little girl," Gus drawled. "Maybe we can fix that. How about a ride on that mare you've been wanting?"

With a sharp intake of her breath, she exclaimed, "Can I? Can I, Gus? Oh, be a dear and consider it a gift! I promise I won't be gone long," she assured him with a smile.

With a wave, she rode off with no conscious thought of where she was headed. The town with its bustling activity and crowded buildings faded from view and the landscape lost the signs of civilization as the woods and brush reclaimed their domain.

How she had missed this! Her depression lifted as she inhaled the sweet smell of flowering vines encroaching upon glades of grass and the pungent odor of last year's leaves rotting beneath enormous trees.

This was where she belonged! She hadn't given much thought to where she would ride to, but now in her heart she knew there was only one place to go.

Home!

The afternoon had given way to dusk and Rachel had just come in from the field. Lighting the candles on the mantel of the cabin, she was startled to see the door burst open and an angry Ransom looming in the doorway, the dancing candlelight casting ominous shadows on his face.

She never heard him ride up.

Her hand went to her throat as she drew in a sharp breath. She was so glad to be home, she hadn't given any thought to her guardians.

At first, Ransom nearly fell on her, his relief was so great.

Then: muscles jerking in his jaws, he said hoarsely, "Do you realize everyone is worried sick about you? Mother is about to have a nervous breakdown. James and Will have been out scouring the town and I have been about out of my mind wondering where you were!"

The ruckus she had caused suddenly dawned on her. "I—I'm sorry. I didn't think."

"Didn't think!" he exploded. "Couldn't you have at least left a note?"

Casting down her eyes, she spread wide her hands and tried to explain. "I never intended to come here. I borrowed the mare from Gus and just found myself riding here. I guess I was homesick."

He stepped into the room and dropped his head in frustration. He had imagined every possible scenario, thinking something had happened to her. So frustrated had he been these last few weeks with emotions that vacillated between hurt, bewilderment, confusion, and desire, he had at last reached the breaking point.

"Put those candles out!" Ransom ordered roughly. "We're going!"

The scene that played in her mind saw the family angry at her, Will with his temper and Elizabeth upset. She wasn't ready to face them and began to tremble. Maybe she could postpone all of that until tomorrow.

"But it's dark now. It would be hard to see," she wailed. "Couldn't we leave in the morning?"

Giving her a scathing look, he said, "I thought you weren't afraid of the dark! It doesn't matter. You're going back tonight if I have to drag you every step of the way!"

Ransom didn't say a word on the way back to town. She searched her mind for something to say that would smooth his ruffled emotions, but no words came to her.

The silence reminded her of her last trip with Pa. He had left her and now Ransom had left her too, at least emotionally. She was filled with an overwhelming sense of aloneness.

Jacob, Elizabeth, Will, and James were waiting for them when they arrived at the parsonage. Elizabeth rushed to her with relief on her face and put her arms around her. Will was irate, while James seemed to take her story in stride. Jacob and Elizabeth, much to Ransom's surprise, seemed less inclined to chastise her. They knew she had not been herself of late and saw her little excursion as an attempt to find some peace.

"You didn't know it, Rachel, but we had a party all planned for you tonight," Elizabeth said with a slight smile.

As her face fell, Rachel lamented, "Oh! I'm so sorry! How can I ever make it up to you?"

Crossing to her, Elizabeth embraced her again and assured her the party would wait until tomorrow.

Ransom, however, was still formidable. How could Father and Mother act so nonchalant about this? Mother had been distracted to tears and now she was so calm?

His nerves were still strained, as he had feared that something even worse might have happened to her. If she was not sixteen, he would have taken her over his knee himself.

Escaping to the kitchen, he fixed something to eat and took it out back and sat in the dark until the family had retired to bed.

Ransom woke with a start as he heard Rachel cry out.

That night, horrifying dreams tormented her sleep. Her dreams were filled with engulfing darkness in which she called out to Ransom. But Ransom wasn't there. He had left her, and Pa was gone, too. She had no one to turn to. She was alone.

"Ransom!" she cried. "Ransom, where are you?"

Suddenly, someone's arms were around her. Pa? Was that his voice she heard? No, then, who was it? She recognized the voice. It was Ransom. But he was gone, or so she thought. Could that really be *his* arms around her, *his* hands caressing her tumbled hair, *his* voice soothing her? Coming out of her nightmare, she clung to him, afraid to let him go.

"Don't be angry with me, Ransom. I need you! I'm afraid to be alone."

"Rachel!" he murmured. "I promise I won't leave."

Her sobs eventually abated, and she shifted in his arms.

Relinquishing his hold, he asked, "What were you dreaming

about?"

"I was so alone. No one was there for me. You were gone and Pa was gone. It was so dark, and someone was chasing me. I could not see who it was. I kept calling and calling you, but you didn't come…you didn't come."

"Well, I'm here now," he said softly.

Pushing herself to sit up, she sniffed. "Ransom, I'm going to miss you when you're gone."

His heart gave a leap at that. Was that wistfulness in her voice an indication she had feelings for him? She hadn't said she loved him but was it possible there was more than friendship?

"Miss me?" he asked with a glimmer of hope.

"Oh, yes. You've been there for me when I've needed you. I—I never really had a chance to have friends when growing up. I guess I've come to count on you more than I realized. When I thought I had lost you as a friend—well, it was more than I could stand."

His hopes were dashed and after a moment he sighed.

"Don't worry, Rachel," he assured her despite his disappointment. "I'm still your friend."

With only a faint moon shining through the window, he was glad it was so dark so she could not see his face. He was struggling with thoughts of canceling his university plans and staying with her. He wanted to take care of her and be there for her. His heart said to stay, but the sensible side of him bade him to leave.

If only she loved him—if only….

CHAPTER THIRTY-FIVE

RANSOM SETTLED INTO LIFE AT THE UNIVERSITY. As the weeks sped by, he quickly became friends with Sam Spencer and Tom McClelland. They were all aspiring ministers and met regularly to discuss scripture and their ambitions of becoming ordained.

Sam and Tom, both twenty-four and in their last year of university, had come from the same county in Virginia. Sam's father was firmly ensconced in politics of the state, in the House of Representatives. Sam vacillated between practicing law and preaching and considered doing both. Tom's mind was firmly made up. He would be an attorney *and* minister.

Rachel was never far from Ransom's thoughts. Her raven-black hair and dark eyes were ensconced in his memory and she haunted him in his dreams. It was the same dream over and over.

In his dream, Rachel walked toward him, a sweet smile on her face, hands extended toward him. He reached out to her and suddenly she was gone, snatched away like a wisp of straw in the wind! He would be wrenched from sleep and awake clawing the air. Dry-mouthed and frightened, each time he would tell himself that it was only a dream.

As she stood with his family to say goodbye, he'd had an overwhelming desire to take her in his arms and kiss her. He had given her a friendly hug instead and told her to stay well. Turning to Will, his eyes spoke volumes as he whispered, "Take care of her for me."

An inexplicably sad feeling rose within Will as he replied, "I'll try."

Every dark-haired girl Ransom encountered was a reminder of the girl he had left behind, and he often expected to see her face instead of the face of a stranger.

It was as though she was there with him, a shadowy figure that followed him everywhere. He was in love with her, that he could no longer deny.

Their last two weeks together had been both an agony and ecstasy. He longed to reach out to her and tell her how he felt and just the touch of her hand was almost enough to cause him to forget ministry as his goal. He tried to play it light, but there was a fire burning inside him that he was silently forced to acknowledge.

Sam and Ransom sat in front of the hearth one evening. It was early fall and the enveloping warmth of the fireplace coaxed them to reveal their innermost thoughts. Women and ministry became the topic of discussion. Sam admitted to an attraction he had to a girl back in his hometown.

"I thought about proposing to her, but felt I wasn't ready for marriage yet." With a sigh he went on, "She'll probably find someone and have two or three kids before I'm ready. Well, I'm not really in any hurry," Sam said with a laugh. "So, I guess I'm not really in love with her after all. What about you Ransom—ever been in love?"

"I not just have been—but I am," Ransom confessed.

Sam's eyebrows rose, his curiosity aroused. "Really! Tell me more!"

Glad to have someone to talk to, Ransom didn't realize his face had softened. Rambling on without stopping for some time, he suddenly became embarrassed as he realized he had told Sam things he had told no one else.

Sam gazed at him intently. "Brother, have you got it bad! Tell me: why didn't you marry the girl?"

Ransom shrugged his shoulders. "She's so different, I felt she just wouldn't fit in as a minister's wife."

"So, who cares? For a girl like that—I would go through just about anything. I don't mean to offend you, but has anyone told you that you care too much about what people think?"

"Now, Sam. It *does* matter what people think. You, of all people, should know that since your father is in politics."

"No, I don't know that," he argued. "If I spent my time worrying what people thought about me, I wouldn't be worth an owl's hoot. Have you ever considered that maybe—just maybe it was God that put her in your path?"

"Sure, I have, but I figured I was just a mentor to her."

Rolling his eyes, Sam laughed, "Mentor! Oh, don't get me wrong. I'm sure you helped the girl. But I'm telling you, I believe that God has a greater purpose than you can see, and I think it's high time you started to look for it."

Sam threw up his hands. "But I know it's none of my business. I'll tell you something though, women you feel that way about don't come along very often and I'd hate to see you throw something good away for the sake of propriety."

Ransom looked down as he heeled his boot on the toe of his other boot. "That could be, but I don't think she's in love with me," he acknowledged.

Sam thought about that for a while. "Does she know you love her?"

"No." Ransom admitted.

As the gusty gales of winter gained momentum, Tom informed Sam and Ransom of some interesting news he had heard.

Coming into their rooming house, Tom brushed thick flakes of wet snow from his cloak. "Listen, men. There's a group from a Baptist organization that's been meeting here at the university. They're looking for missionaries for Kentucky. You should hear them tell tales of all that's happening there. You realize, of course, that the Kentucky Territory has just become a state. Tell you the truth, I've been thinking over what they've said. I'm seriously thinking about taking them up on their offer. They're meeting again day after tomorrow. How about it? Want to come?"

They shrugged their shoulders and said, "Why not?'

No more than a half a dozen students had gathered in the hall to listen. A distinguished gentleman by the name of Alan Kingsley was the main speaker. A vague feeling of recollection passed over Ransom as he tried to remember where he might have met Mr. Kingsley. As Kingsley regaled them with tales about the settling of Kentucky, he put the thought aside.

"To be perfectly honest, Gentlemen, Kentucky's an untamed wilderness. It's full of Indians and fraught with other hardships for those who have been moving westward to settle that land.

"I won't underestimate the dangers that are lurking there, but I will tell you it is being referred to as the land of milk and honey. It overflows with game and cane is in abundance there. Some communities in the bluegrass section of the state are blossoming with prosperity.

"Several forts have been established in other areas, offering safety to those in residence and in transition. We have been sending ministers to these areas and will continue to do so."

Waving a map to make his point, he went on. "However, there is a large, sparsely-settled area south of the Green River that is in dire need of missionary ministers. There is some settlement in an area called Stone Valley.

"Deeded to a Colonel Welling for his service in the Revolutionary War, he has signed over his military grant for several thousand acres to the organization. We need strong, young men for this assignment. You will have to clear your own land, build your own home, and grow your own crops, as well as establish churches and schools for that area.

"It will be rigorous even reaching that destination and we're looking for committed individuals who will stay the course. In light of the circumstances, prospective ministers who are willing to relocate to the Green River area this summer will be given deed to five hundred acres each.

"Special consideration will be given to waiving further requirements for ordination. Upon passing careful examination, if you are accepted, ordination will take place at the close of the school year in early May."

Ransom listened transfixed as Reverend Kingsley described Kentucky. He felt a sense of conviction enfold him and he suddenly knew this was what God was calling him to.

Not some secure, comfortable position where he would grow fat and lazy, although he was quick to add in his thinking, he did not view his father in that light.

But he wanted the challenge of truly making a difference, not only in a largely unsettled land, but in the hearts of those who had dared to travel there and make their homes there.

At the name of John Winslow, his head shot up. Mr. Kingsley was speaking about Rachel's father!

What was that? He'd become a Christian and was spearheading efforts to prepare for the arrival of missionary ministers? He was in Green River country and he would be back to lead them through the Wilderness to Stone Valley?

As Mr. Kingsley continued speaking, he now understood with increasing clarity why he had fallen in love with Rachel. It would be someone like her that could venture to the wilderness by his side. A girl who understood nature and basked in the blessings of earth.

Not a girl with proper decorum, but someone who could dare to be different and would take the challenges of life head on, taming them until she subdued them.

"Oh, what a fool I've been," he thought remorsefully. "I've assumed for years that I knew the direction God was guiding me in and have obstinately hung onto that plan."

Pangs of wistfulness filled his heart. "I wish I'd asked her to marry me before I left."

He took courage as he thought, "Just a few months more and I'll be there to pursue and persuade her until she agrees to marry me, and it could be that John Winslow will be the final catalyst."

If she did not love him now, she would fall in love with him later. That he intended to ensure.

Meeting personally with these great leaders, Ransom, Tom, and Sam contrived to convince them they were the men that would meet this challenge.

Alan Kingsley started at Ransom's last name. "Any kin to Jacob Templeton of Wellington?"

Ransom smiled. "Yes, sir. He is my father."

It was then Ransom recognized Mr. Kingsley. He was overseer in the organization his father pastored.

Alan Kingsley nodded his head. "Good man. Good man. Very well known in the organization." Something flickered in his eyes and he thought out loud. "Hmm…I wonder if your father would consider relocating to the Green River Country and serving as overseer for the churches to be established?"

Ransom was flabbergasted. His father travel to Kentucky with him? His mind began to race. Would Father be willing to leave the church at Wellington? And what about Mother? She loved the luxuries of life, for sure. If she consented, that would take a miracle. He thought hard about leaving his family. And what of his brothers? Would they give up everything and go, also?

In his excitement, his voice nearly broke. "Sir, would you be contacting Father, yourself?"

"Yes. Yes, I'll do so, right away."

Throwing himself into his studies, with a tooth-clenching passion, Ransom tried to will the time to hurry along.

CHAPTER THIRTY-SIX

BACK IN WELLINGTON, Ransom was gone, and Rachel found herself restless. She missed him more than she thought she would. She was working only half-days in the store since fall had arrived. Considering joining the Wellington Ladies' Club at Cissa's recommendation, she quickly discarded that idea. Despite Elizabeth's efforts to keep her busy, Rachel listlessly wandered from room to room in the parsonage, sighing too often. Elizabeth suggested, as she had many times before, that Rachel join the choir, citing once again her musical talent. Rachel took her advice and found she enjoyed it, although singing in the choir meant standing before the congregation.

Rachel noticed that a new man was in town that week and was curious when she saw him arrive late for church. He appeared to be in his late twenties and was quite handsome with a dark, swarthy look to him.

He introduced himself as Peter Brogade and Jacob and Elizabeth immediately invited him to their home for Sunday dinner. This was not unusual for them, for any stranger that visited their church was given an open invitation. Elizabeth loved to entertain, and she was insistent that he join them.

Settling down to dinner, Elizabeth plied him with questions about his present and his past. He came from a northern county, he informed them, and was here looking to find employment and settle down. No, he was not married. Yes, he was staying at the inn and yes, he had been a Christian for a long time.

Upon hearing of past employment at lumber mills, Elizabeth was enthused.

"Peter, our son William has a mill and a furniture store. With our youngest son Ransom gone to the university, it has thrown Will shorthanded with only his brother James to help with the mill."

Jacob tried to get her attention to silence her, but she was heedless of his overtures.

"Of course, Rachel, along with my daughter-in-law Cissa, runs the store. But it is difficult for Will since he is overseeing it all. I'm sure he would hire you on if you would talk to him."

Though most of his conversation was spent with Jacob and Elizabeth, it was Rachel who drew his interest.

"So…you work in the store?" he asked, a smile drawing across his lips.

"Ye—Yes." There was a sudden flutter in her heart as his brown eyes studied her face.

Turning his attention back to Elizabeth, he remarked, "I think I'd like that. Is your son available this afternoon?"

"Oh, yes."

Elizabeth promptly gave him directions to Will's home.

Pleased with herself, thinking she had solved her son's problem, she turned to see a disapproving look in Jacob's eyes.

Leaving the Templeton Store the next day, Rachel heard someone call.

"Miss Rachel!"

Startled, she turned and saw Peter Brogade hurrying toward her.

"Let me carry those packages for you. You shouldn't be carrying a heavy load."

"They're just some yards of fabric Elizabeth asked me to bring," she protested. "They're not very heavy."

"Nonsense. Allow me to be a gentleman and assist you." He reached out and took them from her.

As his fingers brushed hers, the contact sent a strange shock of awareness through her, a reaction that flustered her. Why should a stranger make her feel this way when he is so obviously different than she?

Fashionable, she was not. While he: impeccably dressed in fawn-colored trousers and butter-cream frockcoat. And debonair.

Jolting her from her thoughts, Peter said, "I would be remiss if I did not mention how much I enjoyed dinner at your home yesterday. Perhaps you can enlighten me on something…if I may speak plainly, that is."

She nodded. "By all means."

"Why do you call your mother by her first name?"

"Elizabeth? Elizabeth is not my mother," she explained.

"No?" he asked as his eyebrows rose.

"No, and Jacob is not my father, either. I'm their ward."

"Were you raised in this town?" he queried as they strolled along.

"No," she answered, and then in uncharacteristic candidness, related how she had arrived at the Templeton home.

Peter's forehead wrinkled in sympathy. "I'm sorry to hear of your loss."

They strolled along in silence a while.

"So, then, you have a farm?" he finally asked.

"Yes. Pa deeded it to me before he left."

"Who's living there?"

"No one. It's vacant until I marry."

"Is that so!"

Wishing to divert the conversation from herself, she asked, "So how do you like your new employment?"

"I worked for a few hours today," he answered. "Um…have you plans for the evening?"

"As a matter of fact, I have. I'm meeting with Roger Earnhardt at the church. I've joined the choir and I meet with him a couple of times a week for one-on-one instruction."

"Mind if I escort you there?" Peter asked.

His question took her by surprise, and she nearly stumbled. "Careful," he said as he grabbed her arm. She felt another shock go through her as he steadied her.

When she finally found her voice, she said, "I—I suppose it would be all right. Instruction is at seven o'clock."

Seeing her to the door, he handed the packages to her with a disarming smile. "I'll be back for you at seven.

"By the way," he continued, "Where's there to go for entertainment in this town?"

She gave him a puzzled look. "Entertainment? The Christians go to church and the sinners go to—er—other places."

He threw back his head and laughed.

"Did I say something funny?" she asked.

"No, Miss Winslow. You just told it like it is," he quipped with a dangerous grin. Then with a nod of his head and a tap of his finger to his hat, he turned and walked away, chuckling to himself.

Arriving at the Templeton home that evening, Peter found that Will and Jane were there.

After extending cordiality to the men and charming the ladies, Peter took Rachel in hand and left for the church and Will and Jacob retired to the library.

A frown wrinkled Will's brow. "You know, Father, there's something about this Peter Brogade that just doesn't feel right to me."

"I know," Jacob responded. "I can't quite put my finger on what it is. Is he working out all right at the mill?"

"Oh, he knows what he's doing there," Will said with a shrug of his shoulders. "I only have to give him an order and he's right on it. But I don't like this interest he's taking in Rachel. I guess I consider her Ransom's girl and would prefer that he back off. Maybe you didn't know, but I made a promise to Ransom to take care of her."

Tapping his fingers on the armchair, Jacob nodded his head. "Yes, I figured as much. I don't think Rachel's in love with Ransom, though. Or, if she is, she doesn't realize it. She's been through so many difficult things these past few months that I doubt if she's thought anything about love."

"She may not have thought anything about love in the past with Ransom, but she's acting a little differently with Peter," Will warned. "Peter is more aggressive than Ransom was. I tried to tell Ransom if he loved her, he'd better actively court her and quit treating her like a sister. Now I'm hoping he doesn't lose out."

With a sigh, Jacob admitted, "I've never tried to tell Ransom what to do. He's been so level- headed, but he's struggled so concerning his plans for ministry. Between me and you, I would love to have Rachel for a daughter-in-law. I think she'd make him a good wife and, truthfully, he'd be a good husband to her."

Suddenly agitated, Will stood up and crossed to the window, jamming his fists in his pockets. "I don't know what I'm going to do if Rachel gets involved with this man. I'll feel like I've let Ransom down."

"Well," Jacob said with a little sigh, "son, things are pretty much out of your hands. Where people's emotions are concerned, there's little you can do about it."

"Well, there *is* something I can do." As Will turned to face his father, he determinedly said, "I can warn him—and her."

Will's first stop was at the store the next morning. Cissa had not yet arrived and Rachel was busily arranging a new shipment that had arrived the day before.

"Morning, Rachel," he called as he entered the store.

"Good morning to you, Will," she countered with a wide smile.

"You seem pretty cheerful today," Will said, giving her a searching look. "Did you have a good time with Peter last night?"

"Yes," she said and flushed a little. "He was kind enough to wait around for me until I was finished with practice. He—he seems rather nice."

Seeing the color that crept over her face, Will became alarmed.

"Well, just watch out, Rachel," he said sternly. "You never know what people are like. You should know that from past experience."

Fear flashed across her face at his remark and she raised her eyes to meet his. Is he referring to Wade Bennett? And, if he is…could Peter Brogade be anything like Wade Bennett? He did not seem that way and was, in fact, an absolute gentleman toward her last night.

From the look on her face, Will felt a certain satisfaction

knowing his statement had some impact. Not fair to her, he knew, but after all, he had to look after Ransom's interests.

"I just wanted to warn you. Be careful who you get involved with. You could get hurt."

Glancing at the inventory before him, he casually mentioned that James and Cissa should be arriving shortly and with that he departed for the mill.

Leaving her like that was cruel, he knew, but he had to take matters into his own hands the best he could and if it meant stirring up old memories, then, so be it. He knew Ransom would disapprove if he found out about it but, after all, this was his little brother.

CHAPTER THIRTY-SEVEN

ALAN KINGSLEY, TRUE TO HIS WORD, contacted Jacob and informed him he would be coming to Wellington. When he arrived at the parsonage, Jacob welcomed Alan heartily as Elizabeth prepared cakes and tea and brought them to the library.

Mr. Kingsley rose as she entered the room and upon her departing, commented on her graciousness. Since she always strove to be the perfect hostess, his words warmed her and brought a flush to her cheeks.

Jacob poured the tea and handed a small plate of cakes to Mr. Kingsley as the men sat in Will's handsome chairs.

"Well, Alan! What brings you down here to Wellington?"

Alan laughed. "That is just like you, Jacob. Right to the point!"

He went on with a keen look in his eyes. "Are you happy here, Jacob? Satisfied with your ministry here?"

Jacob was surprised at Alan's probing questions. "Sure. Our congregation has grown quite large. The Council is considering enlarging the sanctuary to accommodate the crowd and the income has tripled over the last few years."

He peered into Alan's eyes. "Is there something you're not telling me? I'm not being reassigned, am I?"

"No. No. There's nothing wrong. As a matter of fact, I have been talking to your son, Ransom. Fine boy. Has a real desire for ministry."

Taking a sip of his tea, Jacob relaxed. "Oh, that's a well-known fact among our congregation. Do you have plans for him, Alan?"

Alan leaned forward. "It's not just Ransom I have plans for. I came to talk to you about *your* ministry, Jacob."

His eyes opened wide. "*My* ministry? It's pretty well settled here, Alan."

Nodding his head at Jacob, he explained. "As you know, last year in 1792, the land of Kentucky separated from Virginia and was granted statehood. The bluegrass section of Lexington has been flourishing and we've sent ministers there to establish churches.

"There is a vast section of that state below the Green River that is still unsettled, although some Virginians have ventured to establish themselves there. The land is referred to as the Green River Country. Colonel Welling, who served in the Revolutionary War, was given this grant of land by our government. He, in turn, has deeded it to our organization under the agreement that we would send missionary ministers to that area. It's a place called Stone Valley."

Jacob interrupted, "Yes, I know of the place. Our Doctor Stone has two sons that have settled there. He's discussed them often."

"Yes, yes," Alan continued. "We've been recruiting missionary ministers willing to become established on the land that we will deed to them under the agreement that churches be started and when possible, schools. Your son, Ransom and a couple of his friends have expressed their desire to go. I'm surprised he hasn't written to you about it."

Setting down his plate and cup, Alan spread his hands. "Here is my dilemma. I need a mature, committed man to oversee the work there. These men are young. Don't get me wrong. We need strong, young men that are willing to stay the course. We are granting them ordination although I would expect Ransom to complete the requirements under your ministry. We would leave it in your hands to counsel them and give them guidance.

"These are different and changing times and we are desperate for ministers in that area. We will make the same agreement with you as with them. We will deed you five hundred acres and a small stipend to carry you through the first year. I know that Will and James are already ordained and if they agree to relocate with you, we'll arrange to deed five hundred acres to each of them, also."

Stunned, Jacob never expected this bit of news. He had become quite comfortable here and had assumed he would fulfill his ministry in this church until the time came to retire. He wanted to laugh at the idea that a man in his forties would be offered this prominent and dangerous position. Something turned over in him as he envisioned years of excitement and challenge instead of comfortable routine. He hadn't realized that he missed the fire and enthusiasm of his youth and felt its rekindling in the revival spirit of Alan Kingsley.

Alan continued. "I must warn you, Jacob. It will be exhausting work. There has been a lot of trouble with Indians and, quite frankly, Kentucky has been referred to as the 'dark and bloody land'.

"You would probably travel there by a road, which is reportedly only a path. Most of your possessions would have to be left behind or risk being taken down the Ohio River. What you take with you on the road will be loaded on packhorses.

"The organization would be asking a lot from you, I know. But it's not all bad. They say the game there is beyond expectations and the cane is in abundance. More than that, I believe God will eventually send a great awakening to that area."

At Jacob's continued silence, Alan said, "If you need more money, Jacob, we'll arrange for that."

Jacob waved his hand at Alan. "No. It's not that. I've become pretty well set monetarily. I will have to do some serious praying over this, Alan. It's not just my decision—I have to consider Elizabeth. She must be willing to go also. Will has become successful in business and I hesitate to say that he would be willing to leave. James is a different matter. His wife's parents are dead and I am reasonably sure he and Cissa would be willing to relocate. And, Alan, I've come to know and love the people in this town. Leaving them would be hard."

Giving him a smile, Alan said, "I'm not asking for a decision today, Jacob. Talk it over with Elizabeth and your sons. You would not be leaving until the first of August, anyway. Most of the rainy season would be over then and you could travel in dry weather."

Slapping Jacob on the knee, Alan urged, "Come, show me the improvements you've made to the church."

CHAPTER THIRTY-EIGHT

FOR THE NEXT FEW WEEKS PETER ATTENDED CHURCH regularly and met Rachel at every opportune moment. She finally agreed to picnic with him on a Sunday afternoon after church.

Borrowing a carriage from the livery, he escorted her, at her request, to picnic at the river.

Finishing lunch, he lay on his side, propping himself up by his elbow as Rachel sat beside him.

"I'm surprised you got away with no trouble today," he said as he looked up at her lazily.

"Why is that?" she asked, a note of surprise in her voice.

"The Templetons don't seem inclined to let you out of their sight."

"They don't know."

"You didn't tell them?"

"No."

He watched her carefully. "I've been warned by Will to stay away from you."

"Whatever for?" she asked, blinking her eyes.

He shrugged as he looked down. "Who knows what's going through his mind."

His mind traveled back to that conversation, for Will had warned, in not too subtle tones, that Rachel was Ransom's girl and cautioned him to back away. Peter had never concerned himself about the warnings of men regarding women and he had always taken what he wanted. Laughing softly under his breath, he knew how easily women could be charmed.

Changing the subject, he searched her face and asked teasingly, "Have you ever been betrothed?"

She smiled as she drew her knees up and wrapped her arms

around them. "No. I never had a chance for such a thing…I mean, until Pa left me."

Blowing a soft whistle and his eyes straying to her lips, he asked, "You mean you've never been kissed?"

Wade Bennett's forceful groping filled her mind. No, she did not consider that kissing. She didn't know what to call it, other than rape, but certainly not kissing.

When she didn't answer, he sat up, threw an arm across one knee, and edged closer to her. "You know, you're very beautiful," he murmured.

Suddenly, she thought of Ransom. Saw him as vividly as though he sat beside her with his drowsy hazel eyes and she recalled that wonderful day he had spent with her at the farm. Her face softened and lost in thought, she quietly replied, "Someone told me that once."

Jealously swept over him and Peter smoothly enquired, "Oh? Who was he?"

Looking away toward the river, she remembered the times she and Ransom had spent there. This is where she accepted Christ as Savior and was baptized. Soft laughter and quiet conversation had gently echoed on the ever-flowing rippling waters on many lazy afternoon days. This was their special place and guilt washed over her. How could she have possibly brought an intruder here—here where she and Ransom had shared so many private moments?

"Just a friend," she said quietly.

Putting his hand to her face, he turned it to look straight into his eyes, willing her back from her thoughts.

He countered, "I want to be more than a friend, Rachel. I've fallen in love with you and I want you to be my wife."

Rising, he pulled her to her feet. Tracing the contour of her face with his hand, he pulled back slightly and looked searchingly into her eyes.

"Say yes, Rachel. Say you'll marry me."

Marry!

He loved her, he said.

Without effort, her farm came to the forefront of her mind. Oh, how she missed the fields and the smell of the earth as its clods were turned in preparation for planting! The marshy ground encircling the springs of water and the open sky with its fiery sunsets unhindered by the enclosure of buildings!

She wanted desperately to go to home. That is where she belonged! Not in a crowded town where everyone knew your business. Living in town did not diminish her longing for the farm, but her oft-thumbed memories merely grew stronger with time.

Yes, that must be the answer! She could marry Peter and they would live there. Peter could help her get the farm productive again. Mother was buried there, and she would be waiting when Pa came back again.

She focused upon this man who was asking her to share his life.

Did she love him? He was charming and she did feel something more than friendship. Just what…she did not know.

Maybe it was love. But did it matter whether she loved him or not? She could learn to love him. He was her chance to go home. Jacob and Elizabeth would never permit her to go on her own, but if she were married, they could not refuse her.

Yes, this would solve all her problems.

Home, at last!

Ransom's face quietly faded away, then she said, "Yes."

"But, Rachel, you barely know this man! Don't you think you should wait a while and think more some more about this?"

At Elizabeth's insistence she wait, Rachel began to cry.

"What is it?" Jacob asked. "What's wrong, Rachel?"

"I—I don't want you to think that I'm unappreciative for all you've done for me," she explained. "If Mother were here, she would thank you herself. But she is not here, and neither is Pa."

And neither is Ransom.

"I want your blessing," she insisted. "This is what I want to do."

"But you haven't mentioned love?" Elizabeth cried. "Don't you have any feelings for Peter?"

"Oh, yes. He's very kind to me and says he wants only the best for me. I—I need to do this and I'm asking you to give your consent."

"But, Rachel, you're so young," Jacob reasoned, "and I don't think you're ready."

She lifted her chin with defiance. "Sixteen is old enough and in spite of what you say, I *am* ready."

"Will you be living at the farm?" Jacob asked, sensing that it was precipitating her decision.

She had not discussed it with Peter for she naturally assumed that was where he would want to live. Surely, he can see the hotel is not a suitable place to live.

"Of course, we will," she said. "The farm is going to ruin, and I need to be there to take care of it."

They tried every argument they could think of to dissuade her, but she held her ground. After some time, with regret, Jacob finally said, "Yes."

Jacob sent word to James and William to come that evening for some undisclosed business. In the privacy of the library, he informed them, "I want you to know before you hear it from anyone else. Rachel is getting married."

"Married?" they exclaimed.

Astonished, James asked, "To whom? Not Peter Brogade!"

Jacob dropped his head and his shoulders sagged. "Yes."

"You can't allow her to do that, Father," James argued. "You know Ransom is in love with her!"

Shaking his head, Jacob replied, "That's been pretty obvious to everyone but Rachel. I can't keep her from marrying Peter Brogade just because Ransom is in love with her. Ransom made no proposal to her while he had the chance. He felt she was unsuitable—I know, I know" he said at their protests, "but he's been pretty stubborn in his own way and if he's let her slip through his fingers, it's his own fault. You can't judge a book by its cover. You know I have tried to teach you boys that. I still believe God has got a plan for Ransom and Rachel, too, but I cannot bend anyone to my will. I have to leave that to God.

"If I don't allow her to marry this Peter Brogade, then I believe she will run away and marry him."

"Father, I've got a bad feeling about this man," Will offered as he paced the room. "Always have. First time I laid eyes on him I had a feeling he was no good. If Rachel marries him, I believe she's going to have trouble and Lord knows she's seen enough of that."

In one last attempt to change his father's mind, Will questioned, "Don't you think you ought to send by post and tell Ransom she's getting married?"

"No," he said grimly. "She's getting married Saturday."

CHAPTER THIRTY-NINE

IT WAS NOW OCTOBER in Wellington and Rachel had become Mrs. Peter Brogade. The family had gathered in the parlor for the ceremony and it was far from a happy occasion as Ransom weighed heavily on their minds. He was in love with her and they knew his heart would be broken.

Glasses were raised in a toast as Jacob sadly wished them well. Elizabeth fought back tears as she hung on Jacob's arm and the girls quietly attended to the refreshments. Will refused to raise his glass and turned wordlessly away.

He was frustrated that Peter had disregarded his warning that she was Ransom's girl. Never one to hold his tongue, he now bit back the sarcasm that was threatening to unleash its fiery storm.

Peter convinced Rachel right away, amid her protests, to quit her job and discouraged her from visiting the Templeton family.

"I just want you to myself for a while," Peter told her, flashing a charming smile. "Maybe it's selfish, but I don't want to share you right now."

He did make one concession, however. He allowed her to go to church, although he quit going himself.

When Rachel pressed him to move to the farm, he refused, stating his job at the mill kept him in town.

Scarcely was the ring on her finger when he began his campaign to persuade her to sell the farm. She wasn't satisfied living at the inn, but when he exerted his charm, he was a compelling force. He had a way with women, no one could deny, and she had an uneasy feeling he had learned this in places other than church. Any attempt to discuss moving from the inn was swept away by his disarming smiles and passion.

After they were married only two weeks, he quit his job at the mill and became a regular at the gaming tables. The changes in Peter were vaguely disquieting to Rachel, for they seemed to suggest very un-Christian behaviors. Time spent in the saloon met with her disapproval and she readily told him so.

His only reply was a kiss on the cheek, but there was no warmth in it.

Becoming restless one Sunday afternoon, Rachel persuaded Peter to ride to the farm and hoped that while they visited there, she could convince him to move from town. It didn't take long for her to realize he was not interested in living there and making the farm productive again. She had thought she was marrying a man who wanted a home and family, but it was ever clearer that she had wound up with a city dandy instead.

Her mind drifted back to the day when Ransom brought her there. He had understood her, she saw that now. For the few hours they had whiled away, he had become one with her as they walked the acres that were so dear to her heart. He encouraged her to be herself and without reservation had stepped in spirit into her world to unite with her, unleashing his soul to God.

How she missed him! Her eyes stung with tears at the remembrance and she realized he had been the only man she could truly talk to. She needed him now, but he was gone and in his place was a man that, in cold reality, was a stranger to her.

Oh, Ransom, I miss you! her heart silently cried out.

"*Sell* this place?" Wide-eyed, she asked in response to his request. "How can you even suggest such a thing! This is where I grew up, Peter, where Mother is buried. It's mine now, and I was hoping you'd help me get it producing again."

"Darlin'," a mildly, contemptuous look flashed across his face, "I never at any time hinted to you that I was a farmer."

Her voice held a note of pleading. "Can't you imagine any contentment at all being here with me?"

Peter studied the meticulously groomed nails on his folded hands. "The only contentment I feel is when I'm sitting at a gaming table with a winning hand of cards in my hands. I need this money for a stake."

He placed his hands on her shoulders. "Rachel, can't you look at it from my point of view?"

Looking around, he said, "I could take you away from all this. Buy you the finest clothes from Paris, see that you eat the tastiest food, and take you places you have never dreamed of.

"Think about it! Parties! Where you would be the queen of Virginia's society, sweetheart—where men would bow at your feet and I, your husband, would be proud that I married the most beautiful girl of all."

He took her in his arms and nuzzled her neck. "Do it for me, Rachel. I need you. I need this."

As he kissed her, a growing suspicion was taking root in her mind that he had married her for the sole purpose of the money he could obtain by selling her beloved farm.

She pushed away and shook her head violently at him. "I can't do it, Peter. I just can't sell the farm. I'm not interested in becoming the queen of society or wearing the finest clothes."

Pointing her finger toward the ground, she protested, "*This* is where I belong. Can't you see that?"

He swore as he backed away. "You're being stubborn about this, Rachel. I'm your husband now and legally I can sell this place, with or without your consent," he told her.

He didn't bother to conceal the look of utter contempt he gave her. "You're either with me or against me. Either way, darlin', I win."

With a scornful laugh he informed her, "I don't get into a game unless I'm confident I'm the best player involved."

Rachel's hand went to her throat in horror as he coldly compared their marriage to a game of cards.

The truth hung in the air and she could no longer deny it. He didn't love her—had never loved her—only wanted what she had. She felt used and betrayed.

"What have I done?" she thought with consternation. Wade had fooled her and now Peter. Will had tried to caution her, but she had foolishly disregarded his warning.

In such a short time, she had been betrayed by three men: first her Pa, whom she had loved with all her heart, then Wade, with his sadistic way, and now Peter, in his self-absorbed conceit.

Ransom's face floated before her eyes. He alone had been someone she could trust. Was that a façade also? True, he never made love to her, had never spoken words of passion. Kindness and protection from the harshness of life was what he had offered her while asking nothing in return.

But he was gone, she was married, and Ransom would eventually belong to someone else. To someone else! If she had been alone, she would have thrown herself down and given vent to the pain that was tearing her heart. As it was, she lifted her chin with determination that this vile man would not defeat her.

CHAPTER FORTY

IN THE DAYS THAT FOLLOWED, Peter took no effort to hide his true self and the change in him became pronounced. Where he previously had taken great effort to mask his true feelings, speaking to her lovingly, his language now grated on her. He became abusive toward her physically as well as verbally. If his charm would not convince her to cede to his plans, then he would intimidate her.

Rachel felt fear rise in her, a cold and terrible fear tightening about her heart. What could she do? She was trapped in a loveless marriage. Even if she could leave, what would the townspeople say? She had been on their bad side more than once and to separate from Peter now would only feed the fire of gossip.

Peter had on occasion, she remembered, snapped at her a few times before marriage. They had been small outbursts that she ignored. She'd heard the anger in his voice, but had said nothing, refusing to acknowledge the nagging sense of something amiss. Now she was forced to think about it: the disposition of the man she had so hastily married.

Rummaging in her mind an expression she had heard came to the forefront…marry in haste, repent in leisure.

When Peter came home in the wee hours of the morning after spending the night in the saloon, his eyes were drunkenly bright as he bragged about his nightly winnings. "Petty stuff, this is!" he said, pulling his lips into a sneer. He was impatient to play in high stakes gambling in the big cities and needed the money from the sale of her farm to get him into one of those games.

His outspoken rudeness made her eager to be rid of him. She longed for someone to confide in, but he practically had her under lock and key. He was around all day and besides, who would she talk to?

But somehow, she had to get away, even if just to the farm. But even there, she was afraid he would come after her if she went without his consent. No…better to get his say-so than just to go off on her own. "I must find a way to leave," she schemed, "without arousing Peter's anger."

She had not intended to broach the matter after church one Sunday, but after listening to Jacob's sermon that morning, before she realized what was happening, her courage found its voice.

"Peter…I *must* attend to the farm," she said in a rush. "It's sadly neglected, so if it's all right with you, I'll go for just a few days."

"I disagree," he said as he continued reading the *Wellington Gazette*. "You're not going anywhere."

Rage rose within her. "I *am* going to the farm!" Realizing instantly what she had said, she raised her chin, but there was a waver in her voice, "You can't keep me here if I don't wish to stay."

Peter was stunned by her defiance and looked up from his paper. "Something must have happened at church this morning," he thought. He did not care much for the Templeton family with their do-good ways. As a matter of fact, he did not care much for churchy types at all.

"Can't I?" he asked with an ugly grin. "Think again. You *are* staying here and if you persist, I shall forbid you from attending church."

Downcast, she realized she had made a mess of her life. Thought she knew all the answers. Well, her answers were a jest. They had landed her in a snake pit. She should have listened to Jacob and Elizabeth when they tried to give her advice. But no…her pride had always made her feel she could take care of herself and now pride forbade her from approaching anyone at church.

Her dreams of darkness returned. Pa was gone, Ransom was gone, and something was chasing her. She called Ransom's name repeatedly, but he did not come.

Through the swirling darkness of her dream, someone followed her through the fog. Jolting awake, sweating profusely, she realized…it was Peter! *He* was the one chasing her.

Dropping her head into her hands, she sobbed, “Oh, Ransom, I’ll never get used to you being gone.”

CHAPTER FORTY-ONE

THE TEMPLETON FAMILY HAD NOTICED THE CHANGE IN RACHEL. Since the wedding two months ago, she had not visited their home or the store one time. She had grown distant, and the harried look she wore constantly was often the topic of discussion at the Templeton home.

James had approached her after service one Sunday morning. "Are you all right, Rachel? If you need to talk, I want you to know, I'm here for you."

Rachel looked up at him and a little smile touched the corners of her mouth. He was like Jacob, more so than his brothers. Quiet and easy-going, he seldom was ruffled about anything. She found herself envying Cissa for marrying such a man.

Without thinking, she blurted out, "Have you heard from Ransom?"

He gave her a thoughtful look and said they had.

Tears welled in her eyes. "I miss him, James. Does—does he know I'm married?"

"No," with a small shake of the head he sadly informed her, "I don't think he does."

She was awakened by Peter's stumbling about in the darkened room. As he lit the candles on the table, they projected eerie shadows onto the furniture and walls. She sat up in the bed. He was obviously inebriated again.

"Not pretending to be asleep tonight?" His speech was slightly slurred as he looked at her.

Her jaw dropped and astonishment was written plainly on her face. How long had he known about her pretense as night after night she had tried to avoid his churlishness?

Jeering at her, "You think I didn't know?" His eyes narrowed as he lifted a candle to his cigar, lighting it, his eyes never leaving her face.

"You're drunk!" she accused icily.

Cocking an eyebrow at her, "That's the best you can do?"

He laughed sarcastically. "Yes, I'm drunk, dear wife, and I intend to get drunker still."

He walked unsteadily toward the decanter on the sideboard.

She threw her legs over the side of the bed, pulled her wrapper around her, and walked to the end of the bed. Ignoring the chill that she felt, "We can't go on like this Peter," she said. "This is not the way marriage is supposed to be and this is not what I want."

He set the glass down, sloshing its contents, and turned. As he approached her, his menacing eyes traveled the length of her, and she clutched her wrapper closer.

He grabbed her wrist so tightly he made her wince. "Not what *you* want?" His teeth were visible as he curled his upper lip and his whiskey breath sickened her. "It's about what *I* want now, and you *know* what I want from you."

Suddenly, laughing dangerously, he dropped her wrist and said, "In fact, there are two things I want, dear wife. First, I want to know, why you married me when it was evident you were in love with Ransom Templeton."

Her mind whirled as she wondered if he knew how often she thought of Ransom. She missed him desperately, his dancing hazel eyes, his indulgent smile.

But love? She wasn't sure about that. He was someone she could relate to and share her thoughts, someone she felt safe with and thought of as a kindred spirit.

Perhaps Peter was right. Could it be she never faced the fact that she had loved Ransom all along? Oh! She was so mixed up. Peter watched her face like an experienced hunter going in for the kill.

"In love with Ransom?" she finally answered. "What makes you think that?"

"I'm no fool." He laughed. "It's evident on your face whenever his name is mentioned. How bad for you. Married to me and in love with him!"

Silence.

"You were no virgin when I married you," he accused as his eyes narrowed. "I know. I'm no schoolboy. I have been with plenty of women."

Then: "Was it Ransom you made love to?"

Fear squeezed her heart and she felt sick. No one but Ransom knew she'd been raped by Wade Bennett. The shame of that day smoldered in her memory surfacing when she least expected it.

Who had she been fooling? Peter, in his worldliness, had discovered her loss of virtue and this propelled her into panic.

That secret was buried, and no one must know. No one!

Struggling to regain her composure, she finally lifted her chin and declared, "Whatever you think of me…I never made love to Ransom and I've never said I was in love with him, either."

"You didn't have to." The line of his jaw hardened. "Besides," he offered, shrugging his massive shoulders as his mouth turned down at the corners and flicking the ashes of his cigar on the rug, "Will told me you were Ransom's girl."

"Ransom's girl? Will told you that?" Shocked by this revelation she demanded, "When? When did Will tell you that?"

He shrugged his shoulders again, picked up the glass, bolted the contents and replied nonchalantly, "Before we were married."

Why would Will say that? Was there something he knew that she didn't? She wished he were standing here now so she could ask him.

"Ransom has never hinted anything like that to me," Rachel denied. "This is ridiculous! I won't stand here and listen—"

Closing the gap between them, he grasped a handful of hair at the nape of her neck and forced her head up, making her cry out.

"Yes, you will listen," he demanded. "You're right, darlin'. We can't go on like this. I don't know why you married me, but it certainly wasn't out of love."

Now, she was afraid, more afraid than she had ever been in her life. Something told her that Peter was on the verge of seriously hurting her for his eyes showed a frightening coldness. How could she ever get out of this mess she had created?

"God," she silently prayed, "help me."

To her relief, her prayer was answered immediately.

Peter pushed her away from him and his nostrils distended with dislike. Walking away, he picked up the decanter once again and refilled his glass.

"The second thing I want from you…is the farm. You either agree to sell or I'm going to the attorney today to start legal proceedings."

With eyes glittering from whiskey, he said, "I'm selling the place whether you want to or not, for I'm your husband and I have the legal right."

She never meant any harm. Only wanted to go home. Rachel now faced the fact that it was not Peter that she loved, but only the farm and she had been willing to marry Peter to live there. She had childishly assumed he would go along with her, and regardless of his scheming ways, she had only herself to blame.

As Peter slept in a drunken stupor in the morning hours, Rachel dressed quietly with frantic fingers fumbling at the hooks of her dress. She was terrified that he would wake up and stop her. She was determined to slip out to the store against his orders.

CHAPTER FORTY-TWO

IT WAS A CLOUDY DAY with a steady downpour falling from a gray sky. The bone-chilling rain had tapered off to a drizzle when she finally stepped outside into the mist. Shivering from fear, as well as cold, Rachel pulled her hooded cloak tightly about her, and with her head bowed against the raindrops, she walked quickly away from the inn.

The bell rang and Cissa, bending behind the counter, straightened, and was surprised to see Rachel come through the door.

"Rachel! I'm so glad to see you!" Giving Rachel a hug, she asked, "How are you doing, honey?"

Rachel pushed back the hood of her cloak. "I'm fine. I must say though, I'm kind of anxious to move out to the farm," she said breathlessly. "Peter prefers to stay put for the present."

She gave Cissa a sad smile. "I miss being here with you. It's kind of boring at the inn."

"That's married life," Cissa said. "You pretty much go along with what your husband wants, though James gives me a lot of freedom. How many men would let their wives work outside the home?"

"I guess you're right," Rachel replied wistfully. "You've got the right man, that's for sure."

Looking closer at her, Cissa asked, "What's wrong, Rachel? Have you any doubts you've married the right man?"

Tears welled up in her eyes. She grabbed Cissa's arm and whispered, "Oh, Cissa! Can I tell you something?"

At her nod, she continued. "Peter has been pressuring me to sell the farm! I can't do that. I've been crazy with worry."

As Rachel brushed back her hair, Cissa noticed a bruise on her temple. Alarmed, she asked, "Rachel, has Peter hit you?"

Rachel fell into a chair and began to weep. "Yes. He's not the man that I thought he was. He acts totally different. He leaves at night and doesn't come home until early morning. He goes to the saloon and gambles and comes home drunk. What am I going to do? He has threatened to see Attorney Adkins today. He says since we're married, he now has the right to sell the farm.

"Oh, Cissa. I've made a terrible mistake! I don't know what to do or who to talk to!"

As James appeared from the back room, Cissa grabbed her wrap and said, "We're leaving right now to talk to Jacob."

Walking over to James, she quietly said she was taking Rachel to the parsonage and asked him to stay at the store until she returned. "I'll tell you about it later, honey."

Jacob and Elizabeth had just finished breakfast and were surprised to see Cissa and Rachel at the back door.

"Rachel! It's so good to see you, dear" Elizabeth cried. "I've missed you."

"I've missed you, too."

How she had wanted to leave this house before! Spent endless hours scheming how to leave. And now, how good it felt to be back! She wanted to laugh at the irony of it all.

Taking a place at the table, Rachel told Jacob and Elizabeth how Peter had been acting and of his intent to sell the farm.

"I'm so sorry to hear that, Rachel." Jacob replied. "But there *is* some good news. Your father made me trustee over the deed to your farm until you are twenty-five, whether you're married or not, and if I say it's not to be sold, there's nothing Peter can do about it. It's ironclad. John Winslow made sure of that.

"When I found out you were going to marry Peter, I checked with Attorney Adkins about this and he assured me I hold the cards in hand. Excuse me, but that was the phrase he used. Sad to say, but it sounds as though Peter married you looking for a quick stake for the gaming tables."

Dropping her head in her hands, Rachel wailed, "I thought he was a Christian, as least that's what he led me to believe."

Raising her head and wiping the tears from her face, Rachel admitted in a flash of self-knowledge, "It seems that I'm not a good judge of character when it comes to men.

"I'm afraid of Peter and don't know what to do."

"I'll tell you what you're going to do. You're moving back in here with us!" Elizabeth stated emphatically.

As Rachel started to protest, she raised her hand, "No, we insist! To think that you've had to endure such behavior from that vile man!" she cried indignantly.

"Cissa," she ordered, "have James take Rachel to the inn to collect her things. Better still, have the sheriff escort them so there will be no trouble. Come to think of it, Jacob, it would be a good idea if we *all* go."

Jacob had received several posts from Ransom, keeping him informed of his progress at the university.

In early January, his letter spilled over with excitement as he revealed his decision to become a missionary minister in Kentucky. 'Leaving in early August' he wrote and confided that he planned on asking Rachel to marry him and taking her with him. Perfect wife for a perfect calling, he had come to discover. "Please don't tell her," he asked, as he wanted to write her a separate post.

When Elizabeth read the letter, she exclaimed, "Goodness, Jacob! Didn't you tell him in your correspondence that Rachel married Peter in October?"

"No, I didn't. I didn't feel the need to upset him at his studies."

Thinking she had a digestive disorder, Rachel had just returned from the doctor, stunned by his diagnosis. It was January and she was going to have a baby in six months! What was she going to do? Peter had left town last month before Christmas for who knows where!

A baby! Goodness, she could not tell the family about her

pregnancy. She already felt stuck in this town and once Jacob and Elizabeth knew, they would never permit her to leave. Somehow, she had to convince them to allow her to return to the farm. Now that she was married, surely Jacob would not resist her wish.

Oh! What a mess her life was!

She had returned to work at the store and was saving all her wages. Her earnings would buy supplies and seed and if she stretched them, she could hold out until harvest in the fall. Fresh-killed meat would supplement her diet. Yes, if she could work a couple more months, she should be able to make it.

Chewing on her lip, she wondered if she could hide her pregnancy that long.

After dinner one evening Jacob called her to the library and handed Ransom's post to her.

"For me?" she asked with surprise. "Ransom's never written me before."

As she opened it and began to read, Jacob sat still, watching her face.

"Dearest, Rachel. It's hard for me to know where to begin. I must say I've missed you terribly…."

As she continued with his letter, tears began to stream down her face as she realized just how much she longed to hear his voice again. He had always been there for her and she so desperately needed him now.

He did not mention love, but as he revealed his missionary plans, he hinted that he would like for her to accompany him to Kentucky.

"Coming home in early May," he wrote.

"Oh, Ransom, Ransom!" she thought wretchedly. "Why didn't you write me sooner? Now I'm married and going to have a baby!"

As the letter slipped through her fingers to the floor, she dropped her head in her hands and sobbed. Jacob crossed the room to her and handed her his handkerchief.

"Oh, Jacob! Why didn't he ask me to marry him when he was here?" she lamented. "Why would he wait and write me now? I needed him so. I've ruined my life and can't undo what I've done."

She looked up at him with her cheeks wet with tears and plucking at his sleeve, begged, "Please, Jacob, don't tell him I'm married!"

Jacob sat down on the arm of the chair and put his arm across her shoulders. "I know this seems to be a bad situation, Rachel. Sometimes, when we've made wrong decisions, we feel we've completely circumvented the will of God. You may not be able to understand right now, but I feel in my heart that God will still work things out for His glory."

"Work things out!" she mourned silently to herself. "With me married and having a baby, how could God work this out?"

Rising, with heaviness in her heart and defeat in her tone, she said, "I might as well go to bed."

Turning back to face him, she smiled tearfully. "I just want you to know, you and Elizabeth have been wonderful to me and I'll never forget it."

CHAPTER FORTY-THREE

IT WAS MARCH. The winter had been mild and unseasonably warm breezes indicated that it would soon be spring. Rachel was five months pregnant and beginning to show. Keeping herself covered in shawls to conceal her pregnancy, she was becoming anxious, wondering how she would break the news to Jacob and Elizabeth. She couldn't wait much longer, or they would guess her secret. Counting her little stockpile of money, she decided the time had to be now.

Dinner was over and they were sitting in the parlor, Jacob reading and Elizabeth sewing. She cleared her throat nervously. "Ah—hem. I—I need to tell you something. I've decided to leave tomorrow and go back to my farm."

Looking up from his Bible, Jacob peered at her and Elizabeth made an O with her mouth. They were stunned. "You're leaving?" Jacob asked.

Nodding her head, Rachel said, "Yes. I've been thinking about this for some time and I've decided it's time to leave."

"But, dear, you can't stay out there by yourself. It's too wild!" Elizabeth exclaimed.

She smiled. "It's not too wild for me. I'm quite used to it, you know."

"I don't think you should go," said Jacob, shaking his head in objection. "Stay here where we can look after you."

"I can't," she said. "I've got to go home and get the fields ready for spring. Please don't be offended. I appreciate all you've done, but I need—want—to go. After all, I'm married now."

"Why do you need to go? You have everything here you could possibly want," Elizabeth pleaded. "I know you like working in the store. You just can't go, Rachel. Wait a while and think it over."

"I want to go. I miss the fields and—and—well, I just miss it." Rachel's voice was edgy. "Please don't try and stop me."

Jacob fastened his eyes on her with a sharp look in them. "Rachel, is there something you're not telling us?"

Her head shot up. Opening her mouth as though to speak, she shut it again.

Casting her head down again, "I just need to go, that's all," she murmured with finality.

He gazed at her for a long time and then said, "We can't stop you if that's what you really want to do. I still think it's best if you stay here."

Rachel refused to meet his eyes. "Maybe." With a sense of urgency, she said, "But, really, I've got to go."

Elizabeth campaigned the next morning to change her mind, but to no avail. Jacob loaned her a wagon to haul her provisions of seed and food and was insistent that she take Ransom's horse. He would need him when he returned to Wellington, but she was free to ride him until then.

She left most of her new clothes. "I'll pick them up another day, soon," she assured them.

I don't need them right now anyway, since I couldn't possibly fit them. If Jacob and Elizabeth knew she was pregnant, they would never let her go, of that, she was sure.

Standing by the wagon, Jacob placed his hands on her shoulders and kissed her on the forehead. "We're here if you need us. Our home is always open to you, Rachel."

Tears hovered on her eyelids as she thought, *If I ever would want another Pa, it would be Jacob.* She hated to leave him and felt real sadness at leaving the whole family.

"Thanks for everything," she whispered and left with a promise that if it did not work out, she would return.

She was going to miss the store and Will, Jane, James, and Cissa. Riding past the turnoff to the river, she realized she would miss church, too. Pulling her cloak tighter around her, she turned toward home.

Rachel settled quickly into life at the farm again. Four more months, and in July, her baby would be here.

The farm had been neglected for almost a year and she relished being outdoors. Reclaiming her garden area, getting it ready for spring, she felt strength and stamina return to her. She never considered that the rigors of farm life, including things like splitting wood, could harm her baby. Though her pregnancy made her awkward, she felt strong and pushed herself hard to get the farm ready to produce.

Her baby had started to move about the fifth month, but by April the movement had stilled. She began to worry that something might be wrong and even considered risking going to town to see Doctor Stone.

In May she began to have slight pains every so often. "Is it labor?" she wondered trying to toss the notion off. "It's too early. Why doesn't the baby move anymore?" The thought gnawed at her.

Arriving home in the second week of May, Ransom found the entire family waiting at the parsonage for him. Jane and William's son had been born in November and they, as expected, named him Jacob, nicknamed Jake. As Ransom was holding the baby, he asked why Rachel was not there.

For a moment, the air was tense. Elizabeth's eyes began to tear and her lips to shape soundless words. Will averted his eyes and stared guiltily at the floor. He still blamed himself for not protecting Ransom's interest in Rachel, but search as he had—he had never been able to find a solution. After all, she was free to make her own decisions, and if Jacob could not stop her, what could he have done?

Throwing a quick, apologetic glance at Ransom, Jacob told him the news the whole family had been dreading for months.

Married! Ransom was stunned. The breath went out of him and he felt as though he had been punched in the stomach. The hopes he had been living on had spurred him quickly home. Now those hopes were shattered into a thousand pieces. The blood drained from his face and his limbs felt weak.

"Married?" he finally croaked. "Married!" he uttered again. For a timeless moment no one spoke a word. Of all the letters sent to him, no one…not one, had mentioned any other man in Rachel's life.

Odd, that right now he should remember the circus he had seen as a child. He felt as conspicuous and laughable as the clown he had childishly admired. For the first time he could remember, he became angry at his father.

"Why didn't you send by post and tell me, Father?" he accused.

Jacob threw open his hands. "I didn't want to disturb you at your studies."

"Why did you let her do this, Father?" he agonized. "You knew I loved her!"

"Ransom, son, don't shift the blame to me. You never proposed to her and if I remember correctly, you stated many times that you didn't think she was suitable."

His father was right. If there was anyone to blame, it was him and only him. He had taken for granted Rachel would be here when he returned and never dreamed she would so impetuously marry someone else.

In near panic, he asked, "Where is she now?"

Jacob put his hand on Ransom's shoulder and told him to sit down.

"She married a man by the name of Peter Brogade. This man apparently married her to get his hands on the farm to sell for money to gamble. She moved back in with us for a while. When Attorney Adkins told Brogade I had ironclad rights as her trustee, he took off and left her.

"She eventually decided that she wanted to return to her farm and I felt we had no choice but to let her go since she is married.

"She was so adamant on leaving." Pausing, in a hesitant voice, Jacob said, "There *is* something I think you should know, Ransom. Peter was abusive to her physically."

"Oh, no!" Dropping his head into his hands, Ransom thought of Wade Bennett. Abuse! Not again! He felt responsible. He had left her without a word of his love for her. He should have given her some indication of his feelings. Perhaps that would have held her until he returned.

"When was the last time you saw her, Father?" Ransom asked, looking up with concern etched into his face.

"March. The day she rode out was the last we've seen of her. She said she would be back for her things, but she never returned. Your mother and I were going to visit her."

Afraid that something might have happened to her, Ransom rose and said he was leaving immediately to check on her. The horse he had been riding was spent and learning that Rachel had his sorrel horse, he asked to borrow Jacob's.

"Surely it can wait until tomorrow!" Elizabeth said. "We haven't seen you for so long and would like to spend some time with you."

Giving her a kiss, he was impatient to be off. "Sorry, Mother. I've got to leave—now!"

He saddled as quickly as he could but knew it would be dark by the time he arrived.

It didn't matter.

Rachel needed him.

CHAPTER FORTY-FOUR

RANSOM KNOCKED, BUT THERE WAS NO ANSWER. Lifting the latch, he opened the door of the cabin and tentatively entered, closing the door softly behind him. Fumbling in the dark, he banged up against something. Moving his hand over a tablecloth, he realized it was the table. Remembering where the hearth was, he crossed to it and as the embers seemed to have completely gone out, he reached for a piece of kindling and stirred the cinders until a small flicker emerged. As the fire reignited, the room sprang into shadowy light and he lit the single candle on the stand.

Glancing quickly around he listened for movement, but all was still. Was she gone? Crossing to the window and peering through it, his sorrel was stirring in the moonlit corral. Rachel must be somewhere. Entering in one of the bedrooms, his eyes adjusted to the near darkness and a movement drew his attention to a small bed pushed into a corner of the room.

"Rachel?" he called.

Rachel, lying on the bed, feebly tried to sit up. "Ransom?" she whispered huskily. Thinking that her mind was playing tricks on her and that the man that stood in the door was a figment of her imagination conjured up by the fog of pain, she cried in disbelief, "Ransom? Is that really you?"

Something was wrong! He quickly crossed to where she was. In the flickering candlelight beads of sweat were shining upon her skin. He set the candle down and taking her hand, asked, "What's wrong, Rachel?"

"Oh, Ransom. I'm having a baby!" she wailed.

"A baby!" His heart was like lead in his chest. On his wild ride to the cabin, he never gave a thought beyond her being married, never thought about the implications of married life.

"My pains started yesterday and they're getting so close together now." Wadding the quilt in her free hand and grimacing until a pain had passed, she said, "It's too early. I'm not due for two more months."

Clutching the leg of his pants, she half rose and whispered, "I'm scared, Ransom! The baby hasn't moved for a month now. Something's wrong, I know it is. Help me, Ransom!"

He turned to go and hurriedly said, "I'll go get Doc Stone."

"No!" She refused to turn him loose. "There's no time. It's up to you."

Trying to disengage himself from her frantic grip, he tightened his jaw. "I've never done this before, Rachel."

Falling back on the bed she looked at him ruefully, "Neither have I."

His face went white. "I don't think I can—"

"Ransom," Rachel interrupted fiercely, "you've got to!"

Torn between the thought of going for the doctor and staying with her, he decided to stay.

Throughout the night her labor pangs sharpened, lengthened, and intensified. Swabbing her face and arms with cool cloths, he thought back to a year ago to their first encounter. She seemed so young, then. Life had dealt her blow after heartless blow, threatening to steal the innocence of spirit that made her unique, an abandoned child unaware of the ways of the world.

He tried to shelter her as much as he could while he had been here, but once he had left town, a thief had stolen her away.

He sighed. "Yes, it's done now," he thought with slow bitterness, "I've lost her and it's my fault. I should have let her know that I loved her. I know she would have waited for me."

He was here now and, though everything seemed to be shipwrecked, if there was anything—anything he could salvage at all, no matter how insignificant it might be, he was going to try for it.

Never did he dream he would be with her like this now, delivering her baby. He could not help thinking that although she was married to another man, and having another man's baby, he loved her now more than he ever had.

As the dawn was breaking, Rachel gave a last shrill cry and the baby was finally born. As Rachel lay so still and quiet, Ransom thought she had passed out.

It was a tiny thing. As he examined it gingerly, the palm of his large hand easily encased the premature infant. It seemed so fragile. He could almost see the skeleton beneath its skin, this baby of Rachel's, the image of God.

It was a girl.

But something was wrong—there was no cry. Ransom wrapped the baby in a towel, stood up and began to silently pray as he saw the newborn was not breathing.

Stillborn roared and echoed in his mind like the sound of thunder.

Startled out of his unspoken pleas, he heard Rachel speak in a spiritless voice, "It's dead, isn't it?"

Ransom turned to her. How could he tell her that her child was dead? How could he tell her that the one bright spot in a miserable marriage, her daughter, was gone—had not had a chance to live and embrace life with its wonderful opportunities?

He was suddenly and fully aware of his own weaknesses, his limitations. Somehow—somehow, he had failed Rachel and her child. How arrogant he had been! He had life all worked out, but his plans and schemes had slipped through his hands like sand!

If only he had been here for her!

He tried for a few moments to postpone the inevitable.

Then: "You—you had a little girl, Rachel."

Opening her eyes and looking into his, she asked pointedly again, "She's dead?"

Sorrowfully, he nodded.

She turned her face to the wall and would not look at the lifeless baby.

This cabin that held so many happy memories of her early life now symbolized only death and desertion. "Mother," she thought.

"Where is this loving God that you spoke of? I feel like He's forsaken me. Nothing has worked out in my life. Nothing! Nobody really loves me, not even Pa! And now the baby I could have loved is gone! Everything's gone! You, Mother, Pa, Peter, and now my baby," she whispered out loud as she sank into coldness.

Ransom worked all morning shaping a little casket to bury the infant in. Finding a fallen pine, he cut a section of it and hollowed it out.

"I never thought my talents as a cooper would be put to this kind of use," he said as he surveyed his handiwork. "The little girl is not my child, but this is Rachel's baby and I wish she had the finest of coffins to be buried in."

Rachel heard the striking of tools as he worked. A casket was what he said. Poor Mother. She had no casket. Buried in a blanket, she was. For a moment anger flared in her that her father had not the courtesy to bury her mother in proper style.

Rachel lay silent upon the bed as Ransom approached her. "It's time for the burial, Rachel. I've got the grave prepared and your baby is already in it. She'll be buried beside your mother. I can carry you there and, if you don't mind, I'll give her a Christian burial."

She refused to attend the graveside service, but she could hear his voice wafting through the open window as the first burial he performed as a minister was that of her own baby. If there was any consolation at all, she was glad it was Ransom and not some stranger.

Afterward, he grew concerned as she seemed numb and showed no emotion and she refused the plate of food that Ransom had rustled together.

"I'm not hungry," she said listlessly.

"You've got to eat something, Rachel, to get your strength back," he pleaded.

"I can't." In a muffled voice, she told him, "I'll choke."

After cleaning up the dishes, Ransom walked over to her and drew a chair alongside her bed.

"You can't stay here by yourself, Rachel and it's not proper that I stay here alone with you. I'm going to hitch up the wagon and take you back to the parsonage. You can recover there, and we'll decide after that what you should do."

Back to town? Where I desperately longed to escape? What difference does it make now?

After a few moments she turned and looked at him. "Your family doesn't know that I was pregnant. If I had told them, they would not have let me come here and I'm not sure that I want them to know. I've humiliated myself enough with my wrong decisions."

"Ah." he said, nodding his head. "I was wondering why Father let you leave."

Pausing in thought, he continued, "It's up to you. If you'd rather they didn't know, we can say you're recovering from some sort of malady."

Reaching out to her, he said, "Rachel, my family would not judge you. They love you and want only the best for you. Don't you realize they would welcome you back with open arms?"

Disconsolately, she gave a small shrug of her shoulders. "Maybe so. Just the same, I don't want them to know."

She shook her head. "Not right now, anyway."

Elizabeth immediately put Rachel to bed. Ransom had been up for almost two days and he was exhausted, both physically and mentally. Without much of an explanation, he fell into bed and slept until the next morning.

The week passed swiftly. Sunday dinner was over, and Jane waylaid Ransom and pressed her finger into his chest. "Ransom, something's going on. I'm going to get to the bottom of this and you're going to tell me. Rachel is not acting right. She avoids even looking at little Jake and physically she's not right. I know the signs." Raising her brows, she said, "She's had a baby, hasn't she?"

Backing from her, Ransom drew his eyebrows together and looked down at his hands. "I can't talk about it, Jane. I promised her."

"Well, you've just told me what I wanted to know. She has. Where is the—?"

The look Ransom gave her stopped her in mid-sentence.

"Oh!" she said, and her hand went to her throat as realization hit her.

"The baby didn't survive, did it?" Tears filled her eyes as she thought about the suffering Rachel was silently experiencing.

"What can I do to help her, Ransom?"

"Nothing," he said flatly. "Nothing can be done."

And there was a man in Ma-on, whose possessions were in Carmel; and the man was very great, and he had three thousand sheep, and a thousand goats: and he was shearing his sheep in Carmel. Now the name of the man was Nabal; and the name of his wife Abigail: and she was a woman of good understanding, and of a beautiful countenance; but the man was churlish and evil in his doings. And it came to pass about ten days after, that the Lord smote Nabal, that he died. And David sent and communed with Abigail, to take her to him to wife.

That was the Old Testament text that Jacob chose for his Sunday sermon. Sitting in the pew, Ransom skeptically thought, "That may be the way it happened in the Bible, but this is real life. Sure, God gave David of Israel, some other man's wife back then, but that kind of thing doesn't happen in modern times."

Ransom loved her. From the moment he laid eyes on her, he had always loved her and always would. The courting he had planned for his return now seemed foolish. The long hours he had spent conjuring up scenes in which he would gallantly and amorously persuade her to plight her love to him, appeared juvenile.

Now, a woman, she was grown, married, and had buried a baby.

He was scheduled to leave for Kentucky soon and had anticipated that she would accompany him as his wife. He could not expect her to go now, and he could not reveal his love for her either.

In her mourning, she had no thoughts of romance and though Peter had deserted her six months ago, she was still legally married. In spite of the circumstances, he still loved her, only her, and no one else.

His plans seemed to always be going awry. He grimaced and shook his head.

His normally ordered, predictable life had been turned utterly upside down since the day she showed up at the church. He had prayed for God to take the feelings for her out of his heart, but the opposite seemed to be obstinately occurring. His love grew in intensity until he thought he could stand it no longer. He longed to disclose his feelings, but he made no overtures toward her. Not only did he consider them inappropriate right now, but he knew they would not be well received.

Ransom and Rachel were sitting in the backyard in the warm sunshine a few weeks later. The color had returned to her face and she was stirring restlessly.

Ransom recognized the signs. She wanted to get out of town and go back to the farm. He searched his mind for every argument he could give her. He didn't want to leave her behind when he left for Kentucky and tried, without success, to think of a way he could take her with him.

As if by providence, the solution came in a large brown wrapper by post. Jacob came through the back door and joined them. Sitting down, he looked at the package in his hand and handed it to Rachel.

"A post came for you, Rachel. I think it's from Peter Brogade."

She looked at it and shook her head. "I can't, Jacob. You open it and tell me what it says."

He opened the wrapping and drew out official-looking documents. After reading them, he raised his head and looked at her.

"It's a decree. Peter is in Prince William County."

He hesitated, and then said bluntly, "He has divorced you."

CHAPTER FORTY-FIVE

DIVORCED! She was not quite seventeen-years-old, and she had married, buried a baby, and now was divorced! When Jacob told her the news, thoughts twisted and twirled in her mind like a tornado, unsettling everything about her.

What would she do? Who would ever marry a divorced woman?

It was something almost unheard of. She had been scorned in this town for something as miniscule as wearing trousers. What would they say about her now! The life of an outcast loomed before her, for people would ban her and label her as unfit.

Her life was over, and she would have to become a recluse. Suddenly, she wanted to get up and run. Run anywhere—anywhere to escape the situation she was in. Was there such a place that she could go? She tried to think it through but her mind kept whirling.

Ransom leaned forward, watching her face as the troubled thoughts raced through her mind. As she prepared to rise, he put a hand on her arm to stop her. He looked at Jacob. Jacob nodded to him and turned toward the house.

Her storm-filled eyes turned toward Ransom, conveying the message, "What am I going to do?"

He rose from his chair and taking her hands, knelt on one knee in front of her. "Listen, Rachel. Try to understand what I am about to say. I know what is going through your head right now. You're feeling your life is over, but, dear, it isn't."

Not over? It's over before it ever really got started!

Ransom cut through her thoughts. "Before I knew that you were married, I had intended to ask you to go with me to Kentucky.

"Rachel…listen to me. I—I'm asking you to go now—but as my wife. Although it's not an absolute mandate—the organization that I'm representing would prefer that I was married. Our wedding could solve both our problems."

Shifting uncomfortably, he said, “I—I want you to know, I won’t ask you for the present to fulfill any conjugal obligations.”

He wants to marry me? Conjugal? What does he mean by conjugal?

Reading the question in her eyes, “I won’t push you to fulfill the wedding vows in the intimate sense.”

Shaking his head, he said, “I won’t approach you.”

He paused, then: “Rachel, you’ll have to come to me.”

Clearing his throat, “When you’re ready, that is.”

A wife in name only? What kind of marriage is that?

Her head was spinning, and she tried to make sense of what he was saying. She would have to make the first move toward him? Why would he want to marry her, now that she would be a shunned woman?

He certainly did not mention love. A marriage of convenience, she supposed. But why would he, of all people, with his plans of ministry, want such a life? She withdrew one of her hands from his and rubbed her forehead in the complexity of it all.

Ransom went on. “It will be a hard life at first, settling Green River Country. We’ll have to raise our own cabin and clear our own land, but it will be a new start.”

He continued on in the same vein, but she heard nothing after ‘new start’.

New start! She stared at this friend of hers who was willing to marry her, heedless of what the town would say, and take her away. He had not said he loved her but, as always, he was willing to give to her and wasn’t asking for anything in return. No, she did not understand, but when was the last time she really understood anything?

For the first time since the death of her baby, tears welled in her eyes as she looked at him. She could always depend on him and he was not letting her down now. Giving way to the grief she had resolutely held in check, she now laid her head on his shoulder and cried with sweet, bitter tears. His arms went around her and stayed there for a long time.

He could not tell her he loved her—not yet.

She was not ready.

The news that Ransom Templeton was going to marry the newly divorced Rachel Brogade spread through Wellington like wildfire. All the previous criticism of Rachel's conduct was nothing compared with the buzz of gossip now on the lips of even the town's highest-ranking residents. Having Rachel's odd, past behavior forced upon them was one thing, but this was the last straw!

It galled them to hear in the same sentence that not only was Rachel newly divorced, but she was to immediately marry the pastor's son! It smacked of foul play and was not to be borne!

Some of the Council members lost no time calling a meeting to decide what to do. They loved Jacob. He had been their pastor for so many years, but, in their opinion, he had grown lax and no longer held to the religious standards they considered to be the backbone of their church.

The hastily called meeting brought no solution to their perceived problem. Threats to force Jacob out of his position did not sway him and if not for the cool heads of Jules Kennedy and Gerald Miller, they would have fired Jacob on the spot. His decision to allow Ransom and Rachel to marry would stand, no matter how the Council ranted.

When the news broke, Council members' wives reluctantly gathered for their monthly meeting at the parsonage. They would have stayed away, but they wondered if Rachel would be shameless enough to show her face. And that very thing, they wanted to know for themselves.

They waited for Elizabeth and Jane to leave the room to fetch the refreshments.

"Mercy!" Eliza Hardin declared in a hushed voice. "The thought of Ransom, *our* Ransom, marrying someone who is divorced! He had so much potential and could have married any of our girls!"

“And you know there’s been a place arranged for him within our church community. Now he’s taking off to Kentucky with a divorcee!” whispered Lydia Taylor.

With clucking tongue, Beatrice Bennett agreed. “I told my Harold, I think some formal charges need to be brought against the pastoral leadership in this church. We can’t have this kind of thing going on and to think that Jacob is performing the ceremony! I’ll tell you one thing, ladies, *I* won’t be there.”

As they all agreed, Elizabeth and Jane entered carrying trays of tea and small cakes.

Elizabeth slammed the tray down, causing the ladies to jump with a start.

“Now, let me tell you something, ladies!” she said with a huff. “You sit smug in your judgmental attitudes, not knowing or caring what Rachel has been through. And as for my Ransom, I doubt that he could have found a finer girl in this whole town than Rachel!

“Like it or not, she *will* become Mrs. Ransom Templeton and, confidentially, ladies, none of you are invited to the wedding!”

Elizabeth was still fuming when Jacob and Will arrived at the parsonage. Will handed Jane the baby with a look of amusement on his face as Elizabeth rehearsed the events of the afternoon.

Upon hearing the heated exchange, Jacob threw back his head and laughed. “Good for you, Elizabeth! I’ve been considering resigning the church and going to Kentucky myself.”

Elizabeth’s jaw dropped as she and Jane looked at Jacob with astonishment. “You’ve been thinking about going to Kentucky?” Elizabeth incredulously asked.

“Yes. I’ve been corresponding with Alan Kingsley about it. He’s tried to convince me they need someone with experience to guide these young ministers and I’ve been praying seriously about it. It would be a complete change to our lives, Elizabeth. No stores to shop in and I know you love the latest fashions.

“I’ve been discussing it with James, and he assures me Cissa would be willing to go.

"You would have to be completely convinced, Elizabeth, and willing in your heart, before I would undertake such a thing. I'm not making a decision today, though."

Will turned to Jane and, in his straight-forward manner, said, "I've been praying about going too, Jane. As my wife, I expect you to go. I know it will be hard leaving your parents, but I feel this is the move we should make."

Jane was speechless and Will grabbed the baby as he saw Jane begin to fall into a chair.

"Leave Wellington!" Jane blinked her eyes. "We might leave here? Our home? What about your businesses you have started?"

He stuck out his chest and grinned at her. "Don't you have confidence in your husband, that I can be a successful businessman somewhere else? They'll need lumber and furniture even more so in Kentucky."

Outspoken as she was, Elizabeth was unusually silent. She knew Jacob had not been fully contented, but never dreamed he was considering such a drastic move.

Later, in the privacy of their bedchamber, she asked, "Why didn't you tell me this before, Jacob?"

He rubbed his face. "I wasn't sure until today whether I would take Alan's proposal seriously.

"We've been here a long time, Elizabeth. The people have become too complacent in their way of church life and I haven't been able to shake them from it. I'd like, before we become too old, to have some adventure. You know—make a difference. It's become so safe and comfortable here. I'm tired of committees and socials and being forced to be endlessly compliant to the wishes of the people. I want to feel what I used to feel and if it means giving up everything that is comfortable to me, then that's what I'm willing to do. We're still young, only in our forties.

"It will be hard, Elizabeth, and I'll have to have you one hundred percent with me, or I can't undertake this. I'm not trying to put pressure on you, dear, I'm just telling it like it is."

He sighed. “If you decide not to go, then we won’t. Just take a little time and pray about it, but remember, it won’t be long until it’s time to leave if we decide to go and there would be a lot to set in order before then.”

CHAPTER FORTY-SIX

IT WAS JUST A SMALL CEREMONY WITH ONLY THE FAMILY IN ATTENDANCE. Though it was a marriage in name only, Ransom wore the look of a contented man. It was enough, for now, to be able to put his arm around Rachel and call her 'wife'.

As predicted, the town broke out in a storm after the marriage. Never had any divorce taken place in Wellington and it was unimaginable that a minister had *married* a divorced woman. There had been scandal of adultery among parishioners, but never divorce!

Women wept over handsome Ransom whom they had fervently hoped would marry their daughters and only a few graciously extended congratulations to Rachel, wishing her well in her new marriage.

Holding Rachel's arm tightly in his own as they walked through town, Ransom was determined that she be treated with the courtesy she deserved as his wife. She was treated like a bad penny by the likes of Mrs. Bennett and Mrs. Hardin and some other wives of the church Council.

Ransom fared no better, but except for the occasional tightening of his jaw, he never commented.

Ransom thought it best to move to the farm with Rachel for their remaining time in Virginia. At least it would get her out of the direct line of fire, except on Sunday, which he steadfastly insisted they remain in church. He had no regrets leaving the mill. He had made his decision to marry Rachel in spite of the firestorm and he meant to stick with it and shield her from any retribution the church Council might attempt to subject her to.

As they reached the cabin at dusk, he jumped down from the wagon to lift her down. When they reached the door, he stopped her. At her questioning look, he smiled and said, "It's only fitting that I should carry my bride over the threshold."

Transitioning from friend to wife was not easy for Rachel. Without overtures of romance from Ransom, she suddenly found herself cast into a role of neither friend nor wife.

Where she had felt comfortable and at ease with Ransom before, expressing herself without reserve, she was now self-conscious and embarrassed. After all, he knew everything about her, things others didn't, and in spite of it all, he had been her one truest friend.

Now, something she could not quite put her finger on—a line had been crossed and she felt a little scared. She had left the familiar in their relationship and was embarking on something that could make or break her.

As long as it had been friendship, she could walk away. But, on her wedding day, Rachel had committed her body and soul to someone, who, if he chose, could wield her past against her.

No doubt her marriage to Peter had set the stage for her feelings now, as she quietly contemplated if she was ready for another loveless marriage. Too late now…the die was cast.

She had never really learned to cook, nor felt the inclination to learn, but Elizabeth had packed enough food to last for several days and with their stomachs full, they decided to spend the evening outdoors under the stars.

As Ransom pointed out the various constellations, she was amazed at his knowledge. Even she, an outdoors girl, didn't know the names of many of the stars. Pa had taught her about the Big and Little Dippers, of course, but that was about the extent of it.

"You think because I didn't grow up in a cabin that I know nothing about the outdoors? I can chop wood with the best of them and have always worked my hands," he said with a sense of pride.

"Look, Rachel! Can you see there?" as he pointed to the sky.

"Yes, there. Look to the left of the Big Dipper. See the Little Dipper and the star on its handle? That star is the North Star. All the other stars move, except for that one. It's fixed, never moves.

"When we get to Kentucky, we'll build a fine home and call it North Star. I know you've moved around a lot the last year and a half, but when we get to Kentucky, you'll never have to move again."

North Star! She liked the sound of that name. Fixed, dependable, always there. It spoke to something within her. Now if she could just get through the next few weeks, she'd never have to move again. North Star! Home!

Feigning weariness after a long day and stretching, he said with a boyish enthusiasm, "Let's sleep under the stars tonight, Rachel. After all, we might as well get used to it, for that's what we'll be doing soon."

The faintest of smiles touched the corners of her mouth. As little as she understood about him, she knew what he was doing. He wanted her to feel like she used to feel. No worries or cares, like she had been with Pa before Mother died.

But that girl no longer existed. She had been through too much, suffered too much, and the simplicity of a carefree life was gone, and in its wake, the certainty of an uncertain future. Still—she cherished the thought.

Lying on their makeshift mats, she listened to the rhythmic sound of his sleep. The crickets were rubbing their legs together in their mating call and the occasional sounds of bullfrogs from the flowing springs echoed through the air.

Ransom did not approach her, as he had promised.

Sighing, she knew she had a major decision to make. Ransom never mentioned the selling of her farm, but she knew she couldn't go to Kentucky and leave it unsold. They couldn't keep up this place and the one in Kentucky they were going to, and, with sadness, she realized, she might never pass this way again. She had no other choice than to offer it for sale.

A part of her would always remain here, with her mother and her baby. Tears filled her eyes as memories crowded her mind.

"Mother, if you only knew what lay in store for us when we moved here. I thank you for the good memories and I don't want to leave you. I still miss you as though you left this life yesterday. You loved me…I know that. If I've been angry because you're gone, please forgive me, so that I might have peace in my heart."

Ransom awoke as he heard her softly crying. Turning over to her mat, he took her in his arms. His embrace comforted her as he stroked her hair.

"Just like Mother," she thought and drifted off to sleep.

Will was having a difficult time convincing Jane to move to Kentucky. She had lived in Wellington all her life and had expected to see her children and grandchildren born and raised here as well.

"Don't you understand, Will?" she argued. "I just don't want to leave. Mother and Father are here, your businesses are here, and it will be difficult traveling to a wilderness with little Jake. I just don't think I'm ready, yet."

He gave a loud sigh. "Jane, I'm leaving whether you're willing to go or not. I've found a buyer for the mill building. No one else is talented enough in this area to make furniture, so, I'm selling the store as well. I'm arranging for the furniture to be shipped down the Ohio."

He paused, not knowing how she would react to what he would say next. "If you like—I can go on ahead, get settled, and send for you and the baby later."

She looked at him, not sure she heard him right. "You would actually leave us here behind?"

At his look, she knew beyond a doubt he would. She had never been able to get her way with him. He had been generous and loving toward her, but in the true sense of the word, he was still the head of the home and what he said went.

There was a certain sadness about that.

If Will could only realize a woman likes to feel that her man can't live without her, whether it's true or not, she thought bitterly. *One day he will learn, and it may be the hard way.*

CHAPTER FORTY-SEVEN

RANSOM WORKED AS HARD ON THE FARM AS THOUGH HE INTENDED TO STAY.

Rachel was confused about that. "I'm putting up the farm for sale," she had told him. In fact, that was her intention the next time they went to town.

He worked like a man driven to tire himself out and give him an excuse to stay away from her. It was difficult living with her in close, unguarded, proximity without claiming his marital rights.

Often, at the end of the day, he was thoroughly exhausted and after eating supper would retire to bed and fall immediately into a deep sleep.

He had made her a promise not to approach her and he intended to stick to it.

When the marriage was a week old, he was mending some fence when she came walking across the field carrying a bucket of water. He had stripped off his shirt as the sun beat upon him, causing him to sweat.

She looked at him in admiration. She had never seen him without a shirt, and his torso showed hard muscle flexing with each stroke as he hewed new rails of fence.

Without saying a word, she filled the gourd with water and handed it to him.

Rubbing the back of his hand across his forehead, "Ah…thanks," he said gratefully. He tilted the dipper, drew a deep breath and drank swiftly then, dipped it again and poured water over his head to cool himself before he handed it back to her.

She hadn't much of a chance to talk to him and his avoidance of her was beginning to wear thin.

"Ransom, I'd like to go to town tomorrow, if that's agreeable with you," she said. "I feel I shouldn't wait any longer to ask Jacob to find a buyer for the farm."

"That's up to you," he said, wiping the water from his face.

Without warning, swift anger stirred and her eyes turned black. She set the bucket down with a thud and water sloshed over the rim. She put her hands on her hips and tossed back her head.

"I don't understand you, Ransom Templeton! We're leaving for Kentucky and you couldn't care less whether I get this farm sold! You're working like we're going to stay here forever, and you act as though you don't want to be around me!

"If you're sorry you married me," she continued heatedly, "just let me know."

Rushing on, heedless of the consequences, she blurted, "And if you want to divorce me like Peter did, then go ahead!"

He looked at her with a sudden, hard line to his jaw. It was putting a strain on him just to be near her. He gazed at her mouth as if deep in thought.

Then: "I guess there's only one way to curb that tongue!"

Pulling her to him, he lowered his head and kissed her for the first time since their eventful meeting over a year ago. He was shaking as though trapped in a windstorm as he claimed her lips again and again, parting them in his sweeping passion, and she became lost in the intensity of those kisses.

With a suddenness that startled her, he pushed her away from him and stomped off across the field. Leaving her wide-eyed, he quickly stepped to the river that ran along the back of the farm and without stopping to take off trousers or boots, dived in.

He was silent as they rode to town. She was sorry for what she said but couldn't seem to find the words to tell him. She didn't understand him. What did he want from her? He never once said he loved her, and yet he had always been there for her. At least Peter was pretty blatant with her after she found out his true intentions.

"Ransom never tells me what he's thinking," she mused. "He acted like he loved me yesterday, but never once mentioned love."

She still went crimson as she thought about their fiery encounter. *I guess I just don't know much about men. Maybe I can talk to Cissa today.*

Ransom dropped her off at the store while he went to the mill. "Meet you later at Father's later," he told her.

Cissa was glad to see Rachel walk through the door. It was the slowest time of day for customers and she was bored. As Rachel sat at a small table, Cissa carried over the tea she had just brewed. Pouring the tea and taking a seat herself, she asked, "So how's it going, Rachel? Are you settling into married life?"

Seeing Rachel's frown, she asked, "Is there anything wrong?"

Rachel stirred some sugar into her tea. "I wanted to talk to you today, Cissa. You and James seem to have a good marriage and I need some advice."

Pausing and choosing her words carefully, she went on. "Ransom and I don't have a marriage in the real sense. When he asked me to marry him, he told me he would not come to me, but that I'd have to come to him. Do you know why he would say such a thing?"

Setting her cup down on the table, Cissa rubbed her index finger against her cheek. "Well, I suppose he felt you'd been through so much with Peter, that he wanted you to make sure you were ready without any pressure on his part."

Rachel shifted in the chair, crossed her ankles, and frowned. "But he's never told me he loves me. It's a mystery to me why he married me."

Cissa laughed. "Rachel! You doubt that Ransom loves you? Why, honey, everyone in this town knows he fell head over heels in love with you the first time he saw you!"

She was shocked. "How does everyone know that?"

"In the first place, it was plain as day when he first looked at you at the church social. And secondly, he's admitted it." Cissa hadn't had a great deal of pleasure in her life, with her parents dying when she was young, but this was definitely one of those rare times and she was enjoying the moment immensely.

"Admitted to who?"

"To the family, sweetie. Will told him he'd better let his feelings be known to you before he left for the university."

She was puzzled. "Well…why didn't he?"

Cissa shrugged her shoulders as she sipped her tea. "Who knows what goes through the head of a man sometimes."

Ransom loved her! What a shock! And she thought he cared for her only as a friend. She giggled at the thought.

"I guess I'm pretty ignorant. What do I do now, Cissa?"

"Well, for starters," she got up, walked behind the counter, and pulled out a package that held a gauzy white gown smocked with miniature pink roses on the front.

"You tempt him with this," she stated, floating the gown in front of her.

Rachel blushed as her eyes grew wide. "It's beautiful. You want me to wear that?"

"Yes, absolutely! I ordered it for myself, but I want you to have it."

"I don't know about that. It's so—well—"

Cissa laughed. "My point, exactly. You want to straighten out your marriage, don't you?"

"Well—yes. I suppose so," she remarked slowly. "If that's what it takes."

Reaching for some cologne water from the shelf, she said, "My dear, ignorant girl, *this* will put the sweetener on the cake."

Rachel rolled her eyes. "My! Then what?"

"Then let nature take its course—if you know what I mean. Flirt with him."

"But I don't know how to flirt."

Seeing Cissa's questioning look, she declared with dismay, "Really, I don't!"

So, Cissa spent the rest of the afternoon between customers giving her pointers on the fine art of flirting.

CHAPTER FORTY-EIGHT

RACHEL WAS CROSSING THE STREET, INTENDING TO WALK TO THE PARSONAGE, when Ransom came driving up. He called to her and she paused as he stopped. Jumping down, he helped her into the wagon.

"What have you got there?" he asked as he noticed she was clutching a parcel for dear life.

Nervously, she said, "Oh, just some things."

Cocking a brow at her, *She's acting pretty strange.*

Elizabeth had dinner ready when Ransom and Rachel walked in the door. "You two are going to spend the night here, I hope. It's starting to get late and there's no point riding home in the dark. You and Rachel can sleep in your old room, Ransom."

They had been sleeping in separate rooms and the thought of sleeping together in one room unsettled Ransom. He didn't think he could trust himself to keep his control and he opened his mouth to say no, when Rachel broke in with a resounding "Yes!", adding sweetly, "Thank you, Elizabeth."

With his mouth ajar, he looked at her and for once, since they had met, he couldn't fathom what was going through her mind.

"I—I need to talk to Jacob about selling my farm," she explained to him innocently.

Everything was going better than she expected. She had wondered how she could get him in a bedroom with her and the solution had fallen right into her lap.

"Oh!" said Jacob. "You've decided to sell the farm. That's good. I've got a buyer in mind and I think he'll give you a good price."

After Ransom had exhausted every subject he could possibly think of with Jacob, the clock in the parlor finally chimed twelve. He had sent Rachel to bed an hour ago when Elizabeth announced she was ready.

Jacob yawned and said, "Son, it's been good catching up on things with you, but I'm tired and think I'll retire. Are you coming?"

He hesitated. "Not just yet, Father. I'll go in a few minutes."

Rachel changed into the gown Cissa had insisted she wear. She reached for the cologne water and walked to the mirror to dab some behind her ears. Staring at her reflection, her courage nearly failed her. She had never worn any nightgown this fine before and it would take some getting used to.

Filled with nervous energy, she began to pace the floor waiting for Ransom to come to bed. Every few minutes she would open the bedroom door a crack—careful of the creak it made and was disappointed as she heard the murmuring of voices in the parlor.

She glanced at the clock on the mantel for the hundredth time and saw it finally had reached midnight. After what seemed an eternity of waiting, she heard footsteps coming up the stairs. Her heart began to race as she expected Ransom to open their door and walk in.

The steps went on down the hallway and a door opened and closed. Her heart sank as she realized only Jacob had gone to bed.

Half past twelve! Where was he? She began to fume and tapped her foot on the floor impatiently. Had Ransom decided to sleep downstairs? Surely, he would have to come to bed sometime if only to save face before his parents. She had maneuvered to be alone with Ransom in the same bedroom and if it meant staying awake all night waiting for him, she was determined she was going to get this settled. He loved her, Cissa said.

Well, she would find out if Cissa was right.

Ransom looked at the clock. Twelve-thirty. Surely, Rachel would be asleep by now. He extinguished the lights and walked with familiarity up the stairs in the darkness. He knew exactly how many steps it took.

Walking softly to his bedchamber, he paused, listening for any sound behind the door.

There was none.

Opening it as noiselessly as he could, its familiar creak made him wince. A faint glow of candlelight was shining in the room.

He tiptoed in and was surprised to find Rachel sitting in the armchair.

Shutting the door behind him and leaning back against it, Ransom kept his hand on the knob. Warily watching her, he tried to determine what mood she was in.

"I—I thought you'd be asleep by now," he finally admitted.

Rachel was holding her breath.

"Apparently," she finally responded.

Rising determinedly from the chair and walking slowly toward him, the folds of her gown danced gently as the warm night breeze wafted through the open window.

"I thought I'd wait up for you," she offered.

One quick glance took in her appearance from head to toe.

He swallowed hard.

"Did you have a good talk with your father?" she asked.

"Uh…yes."

She turned slowly full circle for him. "Do you like my new gown?"

"Uh…yes."

Leaning in toward him, she asked, "Do you like my new perfume?"

"Uh…yes."

She gave a slight smile. "Is that all you have to say?"

He searched her eyes and, in his uncertainty, kept silent.

"Ransom," she continued, "you said I would have to come to you. Well, here I am."

His aching heart wanted her heart's love. More than wanted, he needed it, needed with a crushing intensity to know that she could love him, too. He had waited so long, had loved her without measure. She would never know just how much.

He gave her a long, desperate look, as if his very existence depended on the curve of her lips, the lilt of her dark eyes. To have his hopes blighted this time would be more than his heart could bear.

"I see that," he finally uttered.

Slowly reaching his arms to embrace her, his voice broke as he said, "Come here."

Without hesitation, she surrendered to his arms.

He drew her close and she laid her head against his chest.

Rachel heard the fast thudding of his heartbeat and smiled. He made it easy for her to love him—always been someone she could count on—someone she could trust and who made her feel safe. Always ready to rescue her from any problem or tragedy she encountered, he had given her so much.

And in her searching to find where she belonged, she finally realized her home was a place in his heart.

Looking up at him, she softly said, "I love you, Ransom."

All his reservations crumbled at those words. His heart felt its release and he gazed at her with all his pent up-love blazing in his eyes.

"I've *always* loved you, Rachel."

About the Author

A graduate of Chatfield College and from a family of several ministers, Donna Whitaker has pastored several churches and served as evangelist, missionary, songwriter, recording artist, musician, and teacher. Speaking at various venues, she has also served as spokeswoman and praise and worship leader with Aglow International, the women's division of The Full Gospel Businessmen's Association.

Donna's own family has a history in the area her novels are set in. Of Scottish descent and the well-known Sinclair family, Donna can trace her ancestor sailing on the ship *Loyalty* to North America in 1699 and follow her family's progress from Virginia to Adair County, Kentucky in the very early 1800's. Church and courthouse records document Alexander Sinclair, her 4th great grandfather, as an ordained minister of that county.

On her maternal side, Donna is descended from Brigadier General Jesse Richardson, a Revolutionary War soldier who also served under General George Rogers Clark. One of the first settlers of Pulaski County, Kentucky, General Richardson was elected to the Kentucky State Legislature as the first senator of Pulaski and Cumberland Counties in 1800.

Interacting with people from many walks of life has given Donna an understanding of people and helped to make her an effective storyteller.

Donna resides in southern Ohio.

Donna may be contacted at donnajeanwhitaker@gmail.com.

Upcoming Books in the Stone Valley Series:

The Wilderness Bride
The Lady of North Star
Sand Castles
The Crossing

Made in the USA
Coppell, TX
24 August 2021